MW00779309

ECLIPSE
ON
VIRGO

DANIEL GARGALLO

CHICKEN/AIRPLANE/SOLDIER

Chicken/Airplane/Soldier
Kansas City, Missouri, USA
www.chickenairplanesoldier.com

ISBN: 978-0-9987450-2-2

Cover design: Michael Driscoll

Cover image: Goya, Francisco.
El sueño de la razon produce monstruos.
1799, etching and aquatint.
NGA Images Open Access,
National Gallery of Art, Washington, D.C.
Image in public domain.

FOR DR. KITSCH

BOOK ONE:
THE DEMIURGE

ALL IS ENDED.
- DELPHIC PYTHIA, 362 A.D.
FINAL ORACLE AT DELPHI

OVERTURE

It is strange that those pearls grown for years on the tongues of primordial clams in the chilling sea would fall on a whim to this, our world. They had been picked by hands too clumsy for that realm, but all too powerful for our own. Fastened to metal by a craftsman indifferent to our time and space, they became precious gifts.

She, who had grown tired of their effects, dangled the black pearl earring over his eyes. Erubira tickled him as she slipped its gold hook through his pierced earlobe. The boy and girl had played together in a garden which had grown more beautiful and savage with every kiss. Over-ripe apples fell from the trees, the grass and weeds rose up, and the bushes and vines sprawled along the black-iron gate to the woods.

The boy touched the line of freckles running under her eyes and along her cheeks. She swatted his hand. "Hold still."

The scene she saw in her silver bowl faded as she hurriedly stirred the surface of the water. Erubira's face was entirely different than it had been in the reflection: mature, with pronounced cheekbones, and a wide jaw. Big pallid eyes were devoid of pupils and speckled like goose eggs. Thin and twisting bones coated in a spongey velvet protruded from her forehead. Her skin was a palish pink and she was thin down to her hips, until flaps of flesh rolling one by one down her body consolidated into a tail.

Erubira tapped the water and brought about the

image of a burning blue star. Dim light ebbed and flowed through the single-paned windows into the dusty white apartment. Ivory sculptures of children, clowns, and circus animals cluttered the shelves. Erubira kept a glass case with adorable little glass animals, meticulously staged for a permanent demonstration of life and savagery.

She slumped back against the blue cushion as the door opened. A small man covered in filth entered carrying several plastic bags with him. He wore dirty orange worker coveralls with a blue bandana tied around his neck. Unlike Erubira, Daiki entirely resembled a human in form.

"Honey, I'm home," he said, smiling lovingly at her. She turned over to her side, projecting disgust at him.

He spoke in a low, breathy tone. "I brought you food," he said, and he fell on his knees and scooted closer to raise the plastic bags up to her. "Honey!" he said cheerfully, but she ignored him. He set down the bags and touched her shoulder. She cast off his hand and a strand of her mauve hair fell behind her ear.

The man frowned nervously. "Your earrings," he said weakly, "did you—"

"I threw them out," she said. "They were garbage."

He stammered. "That's not true... I spent years looking for them. You-you said that's what you wanted."

Erubira shrieked and he prostrated himself, quivering. "But," he pleaded, "they were so pretty!" The little man clasped his hands together and raised them up. "Please," he wheezed. "I don't know what you want. I'll do anything to make you happy, anything for your love."

"You couldn't," she sneered. "You're not capable of doing it."

6

"Please!"

Erubira howled in her shrill voice and Daiki scurried off quickly with his plastic bags to his cramped little quarters. He shuddered and pulled the drapes that divided his chamber from the living room. It was a filthy place crammed with boxes and cleaning supplies. Daiki buried his face into his cot and wept.

He opened one of his plastic bags and carefully removed a balut that was wrapped in tinfoil. He bit into it, finding, to his delight, that the embryo was more developed than usual. It was such a pleasant surprise to him that he forgot his self-pity. He devoured it with teardrops still fresh on his cheeks.

Lying on his little cot, Daiki wrapped himself in his wool blankets. "It's my apartment," he mumbled to himself, loud enough for her to hear him. "I pay the bills!"

Erubira tried to ignore Daiki and scried the moments when she played and tumbled with the silver haired boy. She stirred it so she could see when his eyes first opened in his father's arms, his face as he blew out the candles on a birthday cake, and when his mother first introduced him to the North Star.

Eventually she set down her silver bowl and stared at the ceiling. She had spent years under the peeling paint, twiddling her thumbs, looking into her bowl, humming to herself in that mediocre jazz singer voice, so beautiful to her ears. She looked at the glass animals that she loved so much in their cases. More than anything she loved the tigers. If only, she thought as she shut her eyes, if only…

She was jealous of her own Dummy. She wished that she could see and feel what it had. Erubira imagined what it would be like to join that world and to feel the ecstasy of being human. She wanted to break into that karmic sea and tether herself forever to that silver-haired boy's soul. She had never felt such agony in the way their separation had made her feel.

Erubira slithered over to Daiki's chamber, pretending to be hungry. Her index and middle fingers flitted up and down as she picked through the plastic bags of junk food decorated with faceless children and words that never seemed to stay the same. With her arms filled with snacks, she feigned an innocent and child-like frown. She whispered his name lovingly and he sat up.

"Yes dear?" Daiki asked.

"There is something I want," she said. "I just want to try something new..."

ONE

Rain poured on summer's pitched tent in lovesick Missouri. Mary had cut school to see her boyfriend, but she waited for the rain to pass in the old gazebo. She sat on the decaying wood eating saltines, alone. Earthworms writhed in the mud around the abandoned park. Beside a rusty jungle gym, water dripped down a tongue-like slide sticking out from a giant cat's mouth. A few thin dogwoods stood in the distance like little twigs dug into the dirt.

Mary's curly black hair was split perfectly down the middle and yet hung messily down below her shoulders. Her hair felt a little damp, but for the most part she was dry. She had left school under a sprinkling shower and the sudden fall of heavy rain had narrowly missed her.

A boy approached from the rain carrying a black umbrella. He wore a gray hoodie, sweatpants, and an odd pair of wooden clogs. Mary noticed him but continued to eat her saltines, staring at the insect-eaten floorboards beneath her feet.

He was sickly and pale with a pretty and feminine face. His white-blond hair was unkempt and uneven, like he had cut his hair himself. She noticed his odd pair of black earrings, something she felt that her mother would wear. He climbed the stairs slowly and shut his umbrella.

"Hi," he said.

Mary nodded. His feet were filthy.

"You're from Saint Sebastian's aren't you?" he asked, referring to her uniform: a white button-up shirt and a red plaid skirt. She shrugged and adjusted one of her socks up to below her knee. "I remember you from orientation," he said. The boy smiled and sat next to her. "I got sick early on, haven't been to school in a while." He clicked his heels together. "So, you're cutting class?"

Mary moved a tuft of her hair over her shoulder.

"So," the boy said, "you're rude."

Somehow this shocked Mary, who turned to the boy apologetically, searching for words. He stood up and shook his head. "I never did anything to you." He stepped down the creaking gazebo. His clogs beat down on the screeching wood.

"It's not you," Mary said suddenly.

The boy looked back and studied her seriously for a moment. He smiled compassionately, then turned away, his feet splashing down into mud.

Mary watched him walk back into the rain, feeling lonelier than she had before that short encounter. The boy circumvented the gazebo and walked north, up the well-paved road that snaked against the rolling hills topped by the latest developments of gentrified housing.

An unwelcome rush of wind blew through her hair. There had been something warm and uncommonly genuine about that boy.

When the rain cleared it was still grim and overcast. Mary muddied her black plastic shoes as she trudged along past the park onto Calhoun Street. She walked along the crumbling sidewalk that ran by chain-link fences and wild, neglected lawns.

A one-eyed pit bull rammed itself against the fence

and barked as it did whenever Mary walked by. It bared
its horrible teeth and pressed the side of its head against
the hexagons of cheap steel. The dog took a few paces
back and leapt again at the fence, rattling it. She didn't
seem to notice at all.

Countless homes had been boarded up since the
recession. Swastikas had been painted on the backs of
street signs. A pair of sneakers hung from a limp power
line.

Her boyfriend lived in a small single-story house
with a tall roof that steeply inclined into the sky in a
way that reminded Mary of a gnome's hat. She opened
the little rusty gate to a lawn littered with crushed
Pabst Blue Ribbon cans. Mary went up the stairs to a
porch, stepping over layers of flattened cardboard and
junk mail. She opened the front door.

It smelled like a locker room. Fast food trash lay
scattered throughout the hallways. The sounds of Nir-
vana played over a scratchy speaker system in his bedroom. He lay there, that man who had never touched
her, out on his bed, under a Confederate flag, with his
hands resting on his belly like a corpse. Jason had gauges in his ears and an impeccably groomed beard. He
was a man that made his bed and never slept under his
sheets, a man with tremendous anxiety and no responsibility other than a ten gallon tropical fish tank flourishing above a long set of bamboo drawers.

The tank was littered with plastic decorations im-
itating Roman ruins. Three little fuchsia and black
Harlequin Rasboras swam by green algae that had
conquered shattered pillars. An angel fish darted above
a dismembered pile of Michaelangelo's David. Trans-
lucent ghost shrimps crawled along the wreckage like

scavengers in the end times.

Leaving him be, Mary walked to the dark kitchen where the sink was filled with dirty dishes. She turned on the sink and after a second water sprayed out. The scum had latched itself to the plates and silverware. The scrubby she had bought for them months ago had worn out and so she happily scraped away with her fingernails. *Jason*, she thought to herself, imagining him in his rest.

After she did the dishes, Mary cleaned the bathroom. The toilet was stained with a perimeter of ash around the water. As she sat on her knees scrubbing away, a man entered the house.

"What's going on?" Dave called out cheerfully. He was much older than Jason, in his thirties, a short man with leathery skin, big eyes, and a mop of curly red hair. Mary heard him step into Jason's room. "Oh man!" Dave said, and he laughed like a clown. He came to the doorway to the bathroom. "Good to see you."

"What's up Dave," Mary said, unwavering from her cleaning.

"Don't you have school today?" Dave asked.

"Somebody called in a bomb threat," Mary replied.

Dave laughed. "Do you know when Jason popped his Xanax?"

Mary shook her head.

"I'm going to get high and grab some food from White Castle, you want anything?"

"No thanks."

"You want to get high?" Dave asked.

"I'm good." Mary smoked cigarettes but she had never touched anything else, no matter how many times she had been offered.

"Suit yourself," he said, and he stared at her for a moment before walking away.

Several times a month, Mary cleaned up after this man she had met at a bowling alley. Mary used plastic convenience store bags to pick up trash around the house. She put some loose DVDs back into their cases, movies by Adam Sandler and Charlie Sheen's *Hot Shots*. She caught the cobwebs in the corners of the high ceilings with a yellow broomstick. Hours passed as she vacuumed and swept.

When Jason eventually stepped out of his room, she was seated on the couch prepping with her thick SAT math book. "You again…" Jason said, rubbing the hair under his jaw. He slid into the kitchen and opened the freezer, popping an instant burrito out of a cardboard box. Mary continued her problem set, humming some song to herself.

He put the burrito in the microwave and leaned against a narrow archway at the end of the hallway, looking at her. "Do you need me to buy you more cigarettes?"

Mary looked up and nodded. "Yeah."

He sighed. "I figured. I got you a pack this morning at the gas station." He fumbled through a plastic bag on top of his fridge and tossed an unopened box of cigarettes to the couch. Mary took her wallet from her backpack, but Jason shook his head. "Don't even…"

"What a good guy," Mary replied languidly and returned to her math problem.

After he removed the burrito from the microwave, he sat down on the couch, as far from Mary as he could. He took some peckish bites from his burrito.

"Oh," Mary peeped up from her book, "Dave came

by. He's picking you guys up some food from White Castle."

Jason set down his burrito and unhappily finished his bite. He turned on the TV. "Are you doing homework?" Jason asked.

"I'm getting ready for the SAT. It's my last chance to get the score I need," she replied.

Jason saw the triangles and other shapes Mary had copied down to paper with formulas and numbers written elegantly around them. "Do you need that?" he asked.

"What do you mean?"

"Can I have it, when you're finished?"

Mary looked at him curiously, then her eyes lit up, and she laughed at him. Jason looked back at the TV, ashamed.

"Why do you come here?" Jason asked her. "Why keep coming back?"

"I'm sorry," Mary said. "I was just surprised that you asked for my notes. You can have them if you really want them."

Jason had trouble making eye contact with Mary.

Mary tore the piece of paper from her notebook and set it between them on the couch. "I really do like you," Mary said.

Jason scratched his forehead uncomfortably, "I know you're legal, but you're still a… I can't touch you or take you to the movies or anything like that."

Mary put her prep book into her backpack along with the cigarettes. "That's okay," she said, zipping it up. "I never asked for that. Just a pack of cigarettes from my boyfriend."

Jason sighed. "Please stop. I'm not your boyfriend."

"I wonder how I'll look back on you," she said, and she slumped the backpack over her back and left.

Two long leopard slugs hung over the doorway, wrapped around each other like a caduceus, suspended by a thick string of mucus, dangling in front of the door. Mary stepped out obliviously, focused instead on the texture of the screen door. She bumped into them and screamed. The pair fell to the ground as she tried to wipe the grime from her face. She felt caught in some gaze and shuddered as she ran.

Running down the withered streets, she cried, trying in vain to lose the texture of the slugs' mucus from her skin.

~   ~   ~

Who is this person I have grown so close to? That voluptuous woman, so much taller than he was, lay beside him with her head buried into the nook of his shoulder. Her long hair, dyed so black it was almost purple, lay across his barren chest. Her bone white skin complemented his grayish black tone. *How many times have we lain like this?* Andrei liked her, even admired her, but while he had never admitted it, not even to himself, the burden of their secret suffocated him. *This time next year,* he thought, staring up at the ceiling, *will I really be gone?*

Deidra's room was dreamily dark, her bookshelves filled with Alister Crowley's works, crystals, and various tarot decks.

She had always lit the candles as he waited on her bed, except for one tall black candle, which always burned, fitted into a tall glass painted with the likeness of the hooded matron of death, la Santa Muerte.

The light from candles bounced off of stones that played off of Andrei's hazel eyes.

The house was always cold. Deidra preferred to keep her house maintained at a temperature slightly above the frozen food section of a supermarket.

He heard something.

"Deidra," Andrei said, "somebody's at the door"

Deidra's green, almost cat-like eyes opened. She ran a long, polished fingernail along Andrei's chest. The corner of her lips snapped up. "What's that?" She listened for a second, and then her smiled vanished. "Somebody is at the door. Might be Mary." She kissed Andrei and slipped back into a spaghetti-strapped misty black dress.

Andrei put on his shirt and slacks and looked to Deidra. "Same plan?"

"That's right."

Deidra glided downstairs. Andrei walked to the bathroom, running his fingers down his line up. He smelled like Deidra and had some of her makeup on his face.

Unlike her bedroom, the walls of the Sarkisian house were white and the floors covered in a common beige carpet. It was a rather pristine and empty home in its common spaces. She opened the door. "Hi sweetie."

"I need to shower," Mary said, running past her up the stairs.

"Andrei's in the bathroom!" Deidra said, returning to the parlor to take her seat at the piano. Mary groaned and came back down, around, and into the kitchen. "What's wrong? Shouldn't you be at Krav Maga?"

Mary ran her face under the tap water. The kitchen was unique to the house, the only room preserved from its original incarnation, with wooden frames that arched above the windows in the shape of a rising sun and green muntins between the panes. Unlike the other rooms where the windows were typically shuttered by curtains, light flowed freely inside the room.

After a flush, Andrei came back downstairs. "I'm sorry Ms. Sarkisian," he said, taking his seat beside her.

They're hamming it up, Mary thought.

"I don't know what they feed you," Deidra said. "I really feel bad taking your money sometimes."

"Where were we?" Andrei asked, diving straight into Bach's *Goldberg Variations.* Mary scowled with her head wet in the sink. Andrei, she believed, was not perfect, but he was connected to that source that manifested perfection at his lips and fingertips. He had been a student of a Russian virtuoso her mother referred to as "the hag." For years, back when Mary still played piano, she and the rest of her mother's students would see Andrei conquer every competition.

It was obscene, Mary felt, that a boy as delicate and pretty as Andrei was not bullied at her school, but rather revered and left alone. *He has to be overdue on some very horrible thing.*

As she walked up the stairs to use the bathroom she caught sight of Andrei playing beside her mother. *The way she looks at him,* she thought, *what a disgrace.* They tried so hard to never be careless in Mary's presence. The music never stopped around Mary and it bent her to some unyielding knout of etiquette. She was insulted that they expected her to be clueless.

Letting the shower run, Mary stepped into her mother's room. The sheets were in disarray, her "love magic" candles had been lit, and she could smell massage oil in the air.

She caught the glitter of gold on her mother's nightstand. It was Andrei's chain, one he had always worn to school. Mary picked it up and wrapped it around her fingers, raising it to the flame to watch the light shine across it.

When Mary did enter the shower, she donned it around her neck. Once fastened, it slid down to her chest. *What a gift*, she thought. *What could I do with this?*

~ ~ ~

After his piano lesson, Andrei drove home. It had started to rain again. Andrei's phone was connected to his speakers and he looked away from the road, struggling to find a song that reflected how he felt.

He turned off the stereo. His windshield wipers swept at the rain and something in their rhythm suited his mood. The car splashed through water pooling at the side of the road.

When will I remember this moment? He imagined accidentally stepping into a puddle on a rainy day in Berlin or perhaps on a hike on a cold wet morning in the Black Forest.

Once, he had lain beside Deidra and she had described to him the streets of Central Europe in the days when punk and electronic hummed together in experimental revolution. "Atari Teenage Riot," she had said, "there was nothing like seeing them live." He had listened to her talk about clubs and street fashions, but strangely it had been her Bavarian landlady's green wool sweater that Andrei could feel in that moment as his hands turned the steering wheel.

Andrei parked in his spot by an oak tree on his family's front lawn. He looked at himself in the rearview mirror, took a few breaths, and picked up his backpack, hurrying through the rain to the little door on the side of the garage.

Andrei found his father in the garage carving little wooden bears. Having lost his right leg beneath the thigh, Henry Goetz had retired with an incredible settlement from his employer. Henry had become fascinated by woodworking, initially building tables and furniture until something had led him to sculpt animals.

Henry was a large man, a foot taller than Andrei, built like an ox. It was doubtful that dainty Andrei would match his father's height.

"How was school?" Henry Goetz bellowed.

"It was fine," Andrei replied. "What did you do today?"

Henry held up a bear to his son. "Take a look."

Andrei took it into his hands and smiled. "There's expressiveness in his face," he said, admiring the bear's friendly eyes. Andrei rotated the bear. "He's not rigid either."

Henry grinned. "You hungry?" Andrei nodded. His father pulled himself up with his crutches. "Want me to order pizza?"

"I can call in."

"I got it. You have much homework?"

"Not really."

~ ~ ~

Henry and Ramona Goetz had painted Andrei's room light blue when Andrei was a toddler. Aside from some bookshelves and a new bed, the room had changed very little over the course of his life. It had really grown more minimalistic, as his toy-chest and other childhood furniture vanished with age.

Andrei had always been a very neat child inclined toward organization. Something about Andrei's nature had left him inherently independent and self-directed. He had a space reserved for everything and so his room was never messy.

His father had built his bookshelves, but his desk had been handed down to him by his mother. It was a simple and common thing, painted white with a single drawer. Andrei had always loved it, enough to stop his father from building him a new desk, much to the surprise of his parents. Displaying attachments to objects was notably unusual for the young man.

Hanging up on the wall were opened envelopes from a girl called Jessi Lang and some photos of her and Andrei from prom. There were some photo booth printouts of a younger Andrei kissing her. She was a much taller girl with hair dyed dark red such that it came across in black and white as blood.

He loved geography. His parents never knew what to buy him for Christmas or his birthday, so over the years he accumulated atlases and histories told through maps. Above his desk his parents had framed a map of Europe from the time of Napoleon, after the Holy Roman Empire had been dismantled and the Confederacy of the Rhine established.

Of his academic passions, his most beloved was German. Last summer his parents sent him to a German language camp in Minnesota. He often studied on his own outside of class using a college level textbook. Legally speaking, Andrei was only guilty of pirating German films.

Andrei could play piano remarkably well and he aspired to read and write in perfect German, but he had no dream for himself. As much as he loved history, he lacked the imagination to see himself affecting it, and while he thought the idea of daydreams were beautiful, he never had his own.

It was still early in the semester, so he didn't have much homework yet. Andrei eyed his SAT books on his desk. *Mom must have put them there.* He hadn't opened the books since last Spring and Andrei had no intention of touching them again.

When the doorbell rung, he heard his father call out, "I'm in the bathroom, do you mind getting it?"

It was the Pizza Man, a jackal-like creature with curly red hair. Both the pizza and the man reeked of garlic. "How much is it?" Andrei asked, taking a pizza box printed on the top with the name, "Berlusconi's Pizza."

The Pizza Man shook his head and produced the receipt. "Dad?" Andrei called out.

"One second!"

Andrei sighed and took out his own wallet. He paid the Pizza Man and gave him a tip that was much too high given what Andrei could scrounge up, but much too low by the Pizza Man's standards. Andrei felt bad when he looked at the delivery man's expression. He said, "thank you," as sincerely as he could before closing the door.

As Andrei tucked the few dollars he had left into his wallet, his father emerged into the kitchen.

"Smells good, doesn't it?" his father said.

"I thought mom said she didn't want us to order from Berlusconi's anymore," Andrei said, bringing the box to the table. *Berlusconi's: St. Louis Style Pizza Meets the Real Stuff.*

"It's under new management now, haven't you heard?" his father replied. He lifted up the lid of the pizza box and a powerful blast of garlic flooded the kitchen like a terrible fart.

Andrei set the table as his dad smelled the pizza in ecstasy. "You got the anchovies on it?" Andrei asked. "Really?"

"It's better that way," his father replied. He stacked his plate and took a seat. "Son, have you given that scholarship letter any thought?"

"Yeah," Andrei said, "I made up my mind. I'll just go to Mizzou." St. Louis style pizza was cut into squares. Cheeses melted together with the bread. Andrei plucked a hot slice and dropped it on his plate, startled by the heat.

"They're the only ones who get it out piping hot. Sorry. You sure about all that?" Henry Goetz asked as his son sat down. "There's more to life than piano. You might like it somewhere else. You don't have to go to Mizzou. Listen, I talked to your college counselor, what's his name, Mr. Knoll, on the phone today and I think you should actually go through the process like everybody else this fall and apply to other places. Just to see." His father stood next to him and piled slice after slice on his plate.

"I don't want to go far," Andrei said. "I'm happy here."

"It just seems like they're asking you to make a big commitment to the piano."

"I think it's fine, Dad," Andrei said.

Henry looked at his son. "A few months ago you said you were going to do whatever it took to get into Stanford, even if you had to give up the piano. Now was that because of Jessi or—"

"Dad, please stop."

"Fine," Henry shrugged, "I'll drop it."

As they ate, his father asked him where his gold chain was. Andrei had been biting into a slice of pizza, and he bit off more to buy him a moment to think, even though the pizza was burning the roof of his mouth. He had forgotten his grandfather's chain, he realized, at the Sarkisians' home. He spat out an excuse.

"I left it in my P.E. bag," Andrei said.

"Oh."

"It rained really hard today," Andrei commented, changing the subject. "I couldn't believe it."

"Hot as August is you'll always get a couple inches." He was wolfing down slices of pizza, long after Andrei had his fill. "It'll be eighty tomorrow," he said, mashing it down.

Andrei became unnerved by how ravenous his father seemed. Henry seemed to have forgotten his plate. He giggled almost like a child and his eyes rolled in ecstasy. Uncomfortable, Andrei tried to excuse himself from the table to do his homework. Henry looked up at his son and set down his food on the plate, suddenly calm. "Do what you got to do," Henry said. He wiped his mouth with a napkin. "I'll clean up, don't worry."

As Andrei tried to focus on his book in his bedroom, he heard the sound of a Febreeze bottle being sprayed aggressively throughout the kitchen. In a few weeks he would need to read all of *The Good Soldier*, though he hadn't started on it. Andrei had chemistry homework due at the end of the week, but he wasn't in the mood to get started early.

He only had German homework due the following day. Andrei needed to read a short passage about Ludwig II, the Swan King of Bavaria, and write a five hundred word response in German.

The textbook included a black and white photo of a king without a crown, a man in a military uniform fastened with medals. He looked up and away from the camera like a saint in a Counter-Reformationist painting. He had strange almond-shaped eyes and a short, almost adolescent, goatee. Beside the portrait photo, the publisher had included a photo of Neuschwanstein Castle, a fairy-tale castle like the one from Sleeping Beauty resting on the foothills of the Alps.

The passage recounted the Swan King's short life, his lavish expenditures on art, his castles, and his patronage of music. Eventually he had been deemed a lunatic and deposed. Shortly after, he drowned himself one evening in a gorgeous lake. A photo of his place of death appeared below, marked by a cross standing in the water, taken during the golden hour of the evening.

Was his death the product of a conspiracy? Was he insane? Had he been gay? The passage concluded that he was an enigma of history. The open-ended prompt simply asked for a reaction, throwing out several questions as contemplative suggestions rather than directions.

Andrei took out his pencil and turned to a blank

page in his notebook. *The Swan King was a strange man,* Andrei wrote, *notable for his preference of fantasy over reality. This is probably the way people are. We all pay for entertainment in the form of movies or computer games and the like, because everybody needs to take a break. If somebody has enough money, it is only natural that they should want to spend it this way. Some people cosplay as characters from Japanese cartoons and Walt Disney built Disney World. Perhaps it isn't so unusual after all. But to forsake reality in its near entirety, somebody must have something pushing them beyond that basic desire for escape. Maybe he was afraid of people or insecure with himself. Maybe he was heartbroken.*

Andrei bumped the end of his pencil against the notebook, stumped. He had communicated all his thoughts on the matter but needed to write something extra. He stared at the photo of the fairy tale castle.

Some notes he had once played came to mind and he remembered all the sunny days. His pencil darted back to the paper. *The answer may be obvious: he must have been in love with some feeling, something he found in fairy tales and Bavarian beauty, and life without this feeling must have been miserable to him. As such, he paid whatever it cost to bring that moment into the present, and if possible, to make it last forever. Perhaps he even cared about his kingdom, and perhaps he thought this was the greatest service he could commission for it...*

He wrote on happily, delighted by this expressiveness so far removed from his life.

~ ~ ~

At the end of the day, Mary took out her contacts and put on a big pair of glasses that made it very comfortable for her to read in. She changed into a white t-shirt and a pair of baggy shorts that her mother despised. Laying on her bedroom floor, she worked on her SAT problems. Underneath her shirt she wore Andrei's chain.

"Mary," her mother shouted from downstairs, "can we talk?"

"In a minute."

Deidra sat at the kitchen table in a gauzy nightgown, drinking a glass of red wine, having finished a tarot reading over a lime green mantle lined with red tassels. Whether it was her body's effect on dresses and gowns or her choice of clothing, when summer came, anybody who looked upon her clothed form would fall drowsy.

"Yeah mom?" Mary asked.

"I'm subletting the guest room out," she said, "to a man from Sioux Falls, South Dakota."

"Mom, you can't do that." Mary was offended more than anything by the fact that her mother couldn't look her in the eye. "You can't let a strange man into our house."

"He's not a stranger," Deidra replied, and she took a sip. "We worked together all the time when we were doing Renaissance Fairs."

"But you never dated."

The corner of Deidra's lip lifted. "No."

That woman…

"Who is he? Does he even have a job?"

26

"Ho-tah Eh-Rey," Deidra said, holding back laughter. "That's Spanish for JR Tiffany and him had something once, so I'd never touch him."

"You mean that?" Mary asked.

"You can call Tiffany and she'll vouch for the guy," Deidra said.

"I guess that's fine," Mary conceded. She stood there uncomfortably.

"Is there anything you want to talk about?" Deidra asked, as if she was uncomfortable.

"No," Mary said. "I'm fine."

~ ~ ~

Andrei often suffered from sleep paralysis. In the darkest times of the night, he would wake up, incapable of moving, and see the shadows dance around. Abstract hallucinations took on the forms of strange creatures, gawking gazes, slippery bodies falling like spaghetti around his room.

On one patch of carpet hit by the moonlight, a woman lay on her knees, completely drenched in black oil. Andrei stared at her. He was stuck on his side, with the side of his temple on his arm. The oil dripped from her body and she convulsed like she was burning. The woman moved rigidly like a plastic doll. She raised her head up suddenly in the direction of Andrei's bed. She opened her mouth and the oil cascaded inside. Clumsily pulling herself up she took a few heavy steps toward Andrei.

He could hear raspy gasps from the woman as she drew nearer. "Seid fruchtbar und mehret," her voice croaked. Andrei struggled, searching in vain for the

27

way to scream. "Seid fruchtbar und mehret euch und füllet die Erde und macht sie euch untertan…" She knelt down beside him and slowly reached for his hand. It slid across his sheets, under Andrei's palm. Strangely she felt neither wet nor slimy, but instead like dry velvet. The woman pressed her other hand on top. "Und herrschet über Fische im Meer und über Vögel unter dem Himmel und über alles Tier, das auf Erden kreucht," her head bobbed with life like a puppet.

Even covered in the dripping oil, her cheeks emitted expression. Her face swung from fear to joy:

SEHET DA, ICH HABE EUCH GEGEBEN ALLERLEI KRAUT, DAS SICH BESAMET, AUF DER GANZEN ERDE, UND ALLERLEI FRUCHTBARE BÄUME UN BÄUME, DIE SICH BESAMEN, ZU EURER SPEISE, UND ALLEM TIER AUF ERDEN UND ALLEN VOGELN UNTER DEM HIMMEL UND ALLEM GEWÜRME, DAS DA LEBEN HAT AUF ERDEN DASS SIE ALLERLEI GRÜN KRAUT ESSEN ESSEN ESSEN ESSEN ESSEN

TWO

St. Sebastian's Preparatory School had ambiguous and unorthodox origins, having been founded by a monk and nun with an even more ambiguous relationship. According to a plaque covered in moss at the foot of a sycamore tree by a creek, they had been closer than brother and sister. Why it had been named after St. Sebastian had been forgotten.

In the front entrance of the chapel, above several rows of candles, hung a painting of the naked saint, his groin covered by a loose piece of cloth. His wrists were bound above to a tree branch. Arrows pierced the gaunt young man's flesh and he looked up into the sky in curious ecstasy. It was a bright painting and it seemed like light lit up his body the way the lusciousness of fruit could be accentuated.

One little-known fact was that the nun had painted it, basing the likeness of the saint off of the monk.

Sólo amor es el que da valor a todas las cosas.
Love alone gives value to everything.
-Santa Teresa de Avila

The campus had fallen by law from an order that had thinned considerably in that part of Missouri into legal independence from the Church as a non-profit organization. That school, having once been staffed entirely by clergy, was almost completely operated by the laity. The monks of the First Order had withered away and the few remaining nuns of the Second Order were women from Europe or Africa more concerned with mitigating homelessness than the education of affluent teenagers, with the exception of Sister Bernadette, an old Senegalese woman who had been headmaster since the nineties, a teacher there since the eighties.

She had seen the school change considerably in thirty years. The board of trustees diversified in beliefs and countless committees on inclusion came and went. She had upset the Bishop and the Diocese incessantly and had spent many nights sleepless.

Sister Bernadette believed in her students and loved them. She wanted them to be happy and free.

Every morning she would look out the window of her office and see the students trudging up the hill from the parking lot, up the dirt trails lined by logs, and she would repeat to herself the name of each pupil, only naming them incorrectly if the child had a likeness to an older sibling or possibly even a parent who had studied at St. Sebastian's.

Despite his beauty and sensitivity, Andrei always seemed to Sister Bernadette like he had just cast off some veil of grey the moment he reached the school grounds. He never seemed lonelier than when he mingled with others.

On that sunny day, when the temperature had reached ninety degrees Fahrenheit, the rolling fields seemed golden. The Gothic buildings built from sandstone jutted into the clear sky. In the sweltering heat armpit sweat bled through each student's white button-up shirt, but Andrei trudged up the hill wearing a tank top, keeping his shirt on a coat hanger hung over his shoulder. Toby, a Goliath of a senior who had sprouted thick yet scattered stringy strands of hair on his cheeks and under his chin, jogged up to Andrei. His shirt was already drenched in perspiration.

Andrei noticed Toby pull up and greeted him.

"What's that?" Toby said, feigning surprise. "Oh sorry man, I didn't even notice you were next to me."

"Hot day isn't it?" Andrei asked.

Toby rolled his eyes. "Pfftt... it feels hotter than back home. I swear, I almost passed out yesterday in a parking lot."

"I believe it," Andrei said.

"I'm tired as hell man," Toby went on. "I was talking to my girlfriend until four A.M. last night. Long distance is such a pain."

"I believe you," Andrei said, noticing that the roof of his mouth was still burnt from last night's pizza. Passing through the entrance, Andrei found relief in the building's cool, dry air. He quickly slipped on his button-up shirt, fastening it carelessly.

Mary stood at her locker unloading her backpack. She stared him down as they passed by. His chain hung around her collar. She picked up some books and walked away. *Surely she won't tell anybody*, he thought, *but why grandpa's chain?*

"Dude what was up with that?" Toby asked. "She was giving you the eye."

"Is that how you read it?"

"Yeah, but I wouldn't get your hopes up too high, man," Toby replied. "She's never put out before. Believe me, I have the pulse on the sex life here." Toby nudged him. "But it's worth a shot. You should go talk to her sometime."

"I should," Andrei said, and anxiety, an emotion foreign to him, welled inside.

~ ~ ~

"Are you kidding me?" Mary asked. "This is a poem
about fucking an angel." She was seated in her English
class.

Valeria Ortiz, the mayor's daughter, had just finished a presentation, ending with a slide showing
St. Teresa of Avila lying on her back, writhing in joy,
clutching her breast.

Valeria's peroxide blond hair, split down the middle
by a phantasmal yet precise line, was kept to a shoulder, from where it lay down her torso. She had thick
fake eyelashes around her bright, green eyes covered
by massively round glasses identical to the kind Mary
wore at night. As pristine as Valeria's appearance was,
her lenses tended to be dirty.

Mr. Miet, a round man with a tall forehead and
thick curls of hair like a French revolutionary, unen-
thusiastically called after her. "English, Mary. Please
explain to the class what you mean with thoughtful
English."

Mary crossed her arms and bent over the handout
Valeria had given the rest of the class. "I saw in his hand
a long golden spear that he plunged into my heart several times, it penetrated my entrails, the pain was so
severe that it made me moan again and again, but the
pain was so overwhelmingly sweet that I couldn't wish
for it to end." She looked up at Mr. Miet. "Do you actually think she was having a vision about getting violently stabbed? I'm not crazy, the guy who made that painting obviously thought the same thing. I mean, that girl's

playing with herself."

Valeria cast a few playful glances at the other students, students with whom she had shared no connection. "I think everybody here gets that it's a metaphor. But the spear isn't a metaphor for sex. Sex is a metaphor for her connection to God. It's that obvious."

"What do you mean it's that obvious? Just because it's a connection to God doesn't change the fact that she sees—feels—it sexually."

Valeria looked at Mary frostily. Her serene disposition was so composed that she prompted condescending laughter from the students. "An angel—divinity as a whole—isn't on the same plane as the physical world of lust. Intimacy with divinity is pure. That's Plato. From top to bottom."

"You're lying to yourself."

"I'm lying to myself?"

Mary fell into the pits of indifference in Valeria's eyes. "You're just coming up with an excuse for it, because you know that what I'm saying is, from your point of view, perverse. You don't want to admit that it's possible that St. Teresa literally wanted to have an angel come down to this physical world and fuck her."

Mr. Miet interjected, "Mary, can you please?"

Valeria stood still with perfect posture. Mary's retort glanced off of Valeria. "Why wouldn't I want to admit that?"

"Because you can't stand the idea that you and St. Teresa do not share the same god."

"What are you talking about, Mary?" Valeria said, "This is Saint Teresa, a nun in the Catholic Church. This is a Catholic school. I am a confirmed Catholic."

"You certainly belong to the same institution," Mary

33

said, "but you don't worship the same god."

"You are incapable of determining which god I do or do not worship. You have never once felt God. You have lived a life in darkness."

Mr. Miet's jaw dropped.

Mary's face flushed red. *How dare you speak in that condescending tone?* She gritted her teeth for a second and stood up. *Nobody talks like that!* The classroom froze around this interaction—it felt like something between them was rippling out, as if a stone had been dropped into a pond.

Mr. Miet rose up and bumbled down the aisle. "That's it. You two are done! I want you out, both of you. I want you to go straight to the headmaster's office."

They moved to the hallway as if being sucked into a vacuum.

Mary opened the door and wedged herself between Valeria and the hallway. Just before Mary could speak, Valeria's words punctured her with stunning speed and grace.

"This can't be going the way you want it to, can it Mary?"

Mr. Miet followed behind the girls in the hallway. "Silence, the both of you."

Valeria walked placidly beside Mary.

How can she smile so insolently? Is this really that same girl?

Two summers past, Valeria had wiped blood from the edge of her lip prior to lighting up a cigarette. She tossed the box of cigarettes onto Mary's lap. Mary clutched her stomach. Her temple had been cut and bled steadily down her face. She didn't know if they had lost or won until she saw Valeria standing so composed while staring out into the vespertine sun.

They listened quietly to the cicada rhythms.

Mary took out a bent cigarette from the ravaged box and flicked the lighter a few times until she got a spark. Her body ached. She would have cried, but she didn't want to spoil whatever her friend felt in that moment. Valeria tore off a strip of cloth from her torn shirt. She squatted in front of Mary and crudely dressed her cut into a head band.

"Come on," Valeria wrapped her friend's arm around her shoulder and lifted her up, "this will be our last free night of the summer."

~   ~   ~

"Yeah man, cigarettes aren't even that bad for you, the only reason people are getting lung cancer is because of the chem trails left by planes," Toby explained.

Andrei was lying by the creek under the sycamore tree with his head resting on his palms. Toby had stood over him for the duration of their morning break. Mary, he had heard, was in Sister Bernadette's office. Fearing that she was spilling everything about her mother's affair, Andrei imagined the awkward conversation with his parents, the unwanted attention from his peers, and the shame that would befall Deidra.

"It always goes back to the Rothschilds, you know what I mean?" Toby said.

"I'm sad," Andrei said.

"Yeah no kidding man," Toby replied. "We're all pawns in somebody else's game. Seriously, once I graduate I'm going to go to the embassy Julian Assange is holed up in. He'll have to take me on as his intern."

A squirrel ran past Andrei's feet. One of the Hmong gardeners was strolling by with a wheelbarrow. Toby pressed his palms together and bowed. The gardener laughed and wagged a finger at Toby. "Where are you going?" Toby asked.

The gardener pointed to the cloister on the hill at the other end of the creek. There was a beautiful hedge garden around its perimeter. The land on the other end was off limits to students and was used as a place of retreat for artists or people with terminal illnesses. He pulled two onions from his wheelbarrow and approached the two, offering one to Toby. Andrei sat up and received his onion from the gardener.

"Many thanks," Toby said, bowing again.

The old gardener laughed again and waved his hand to make Toby stop.

"Thank you," Andrei said. To his surprise, he was enlivened by the gift of this onion. When the bell rang he walked up the hill carefree. Each blade of grass emanated a rich coat of light. Toby's words blended into the sunlight, the wind, the frisbee golfers on the hill, and the bell's toll.

~ ~ ~

"I said that St. Teresa was writing about an erotic relationship with the holy spirit," Mary began. Valeria stared blankly at Mary. Sister Bernadette was flipping through the hand-out from Valeria's presentation.

"I don't think that there's anything groundbreaking in saying that any woman who gives herself to God as a nun is pursuing a union no different than that between man and wife," Sister Bernadette said in a calm but stern voice. "Why would Mr. Miet send you here?"

"That's not what we were disagreeing about," Valeria replied, slightly annoyed.

"So there was some consensus," Sister Bernadette said.

"Hardly," Mary said.

The nun shook her head. "Valeria, you're free to go."

"Are you crazy?" Mary said.

"No I'm not. Valeria get out," Sister Bernadette ordered, shooing Valeria away with her hand. "And close the door behind you."

Once the door shut, Sister Bernadette opened a drawer. "You want some candy? M&M's?"

"Yeah," Mary said.

"Good, hold out your hand." Seeing Mary's reluctance Sister Bernadette laughed. "I'm not going to slap your wrists with a ruler." Mary stuck out her arms and Sister Bernadette sprinkled some M&M's into her hand. She ate some herself, munched happily, and swallowed. "You left sick yesterday. Feeling better today?"

"Much better, Sister Bernadette."

"I'm glad. You used to care so much about Valeria, what happened?"

"You know what happened," Mary said, "and you know that she's not the person she used to be. I hate the Jesus Freak she is now."

Sister Bernadette waved a hand in a circle. "Why?"

Mary folded her arms. "I've got nothing against you. She uses it to judge people."

"You never had problems dealing with people with different views. You were fine during the election," Sister Bernadette said. "Why is it that Valeria provokes you?"

37

"Let's say that this was Spain and she was the In-quisition and our lives were in her hands to judge. The only thing that's keeping her from exacting judgement on us—"

"Stop."

"—the fact that she does not have the power."

"Stop!"

"And even if there's a one percent—"

"STOP!" The nun stood up and slammed her fists on the table. "You're smart Mary, so I treat you that way." Her voice immediately mellowed out. "But school isn't about being smart. I'm going to tell you something that I will never repeat outside of this room. No institution, not even a learning institution, is about truth. It is never about being right. You were right about St. Teresa, but you were wrong about how you said it. You could have said it in a way that wouldn't have brought you here. If you don't learn that basic competency I guarantee you won't make it anywhere in life." Sister Bernadette sat down. "I was born in a different place in a different time. I wanted an education and the chance to change things. That's how I wound up here. The only reason why I was never silenced is because I know how to rock the boat. Do you understand what I'm saying?"

Mary nodded.

"But that's not why I'm disappointed in you," Sister Bernadette said. She sized up Mary's face. "You know why she left. You know what's haunting her. You can pretend that you don't, but the fact that you found some way to blame her is what disappoints me."

~ ~ ~

Valeria found that the kind old man who had taught her English freshman year had forgotten their appointment. During the lunch hour she opened his door expecting warmth and instead met a dark room. She set her lunch tray on a desk and paced around the room, treading across a tree's shadow shaking beneath her. Valeria thought of the Mary from that day and the Mary from years before. She thought of herself.

The old man wasn't coming. She shut the door and slid down against the wall under the whiteboard. Valeria took off her glasses and wrapped her hands around her knees. Her memories of Mary had long ago soured. The therapist's lectures hung above her. Pathetic below them, she wept.

Andrei opened the door and the light from the hallway fell upon Valeria. She stood up in a hurry, embarrassed as if she had been caught changing. Her foot knocked her glasses into Andrei's path and they cracked under his footstep.

"Oh God," he said, processing this image of a weeping girl. He lifted his foot. The frame was mangled and a lens had popped away. He apologized profusely and searched for the missing lens on the ground. "I'm sorry," he repeatedly said. She tried out of pride to contain her tears.

"At least shut the door," Valeria hissed, and he did. "I'm blind," she said, sitting down in the old man's chair.

"I'll buy you another pair," Andrei said. "I promise."

"I'm in pain," she said. Andrei didn't know if he could have reassured her with touch or space. He took a few steps closer to her and the memory of the ap-

39

parition that had visited him the night before creeped within him. "It's not you. I was crying before you came."

"What's wrong?" Andrei asked.

Valeria looked up at Andrei and shook her head. "I want to belong here." The light caught the tears in her eyes. "I'm trying... I hate praying Andrei, I really do, but that's all..." She wiped the tears from her eyes. "I don't know what I'm saying."

Andrei would have knelt beside her if not for his dream. Instead he sat on the old man's desk and looked out the window at the cloister on the other side of the stream. He felt the way he did after having sex on days when he wanted to be anywhere but bound to a partner's bedside. "Can I drive you to the eye doctor after class?" he asked. "I'd like to."

"Believe me, you don't," Valeria said. "You're kind to offer, but I'm sure it'd be better if my mom took me."

He sat there patiently until he noticed that Valeria was looking at him.

"No," Valeria said, "she has to take my dad to the dentist to get a tooth pulled." She dried her face with her sleeve. "Maybe you could take me."

~ ~ ~

At the end of school, as Andrei packed his bag, he noticed Mary standing at her locker staring at him. *She hates me*, Andrei thought. *I can feel it*. Valeria pulled his sleeve. "Is that an onion?"

Andrei lifted the onion from his backpack, still concerned by Mary's glare.

"Ignore her," she said. "She's probably jealous about seeing me next to you."

Valeria was in a better mood, though a little nervous as she sat in his clean little car. Andrei bothered to make small talk at first, to which she was receptive, but his mind was still fixated on the necklace.

"Hey, do you have Mary's phone number?"

"Why?"

"I need to pick some books up from her house and I wanted to figure out when would be a good time."

"Why is she loaning you books?"

"Her mom's my piano teacher," Andrei said. "It's not related to school."

"Can't you just ask her mom?"

"Yeah," Andrei said, "I could, but you're right here."

"I deleted her number from my phone," Valeria said. "We're not friends anymore."

"How did that happen?"

"Don't you know?" Valeria asked. She scratched the hair beside her ear. "Please don't make me spell it out for you. I ride horses and I go to church."

Andrei stopped to consider his words. "I don't know what happened over the last year, but there's more to you than that." Andrei took his eyes off the road for a second to look at her. "Valeria, sophomore year, on the ski trip, I'm sorry that we never hung out after that. That was the first time I drank, did you know that? And that was the only time in my life I ever stole. And we tagged those mailboxes, and... Valeria?"

"Yes?"

"That was probably my happiest day that year," he said.

Valeria cleared her throat. Her eyes widened and she smiled. "That's so sweet of you to say. I'm glad that at least that can be a happy memory for you."

Andrei moved back against his seat. "I guess you don't look back happily on that then."

"It's just... I hate myself for saying it."

"Say it."

Her face turned red. "It wasn't Christ-like."

"Oh," Andrei replied, disappointed, "I understand."

Andrei fidgeted with his stereo.

Valeria looked at him and grabbed his wrist. "Do you think I'm wrong?"

He scratched himself behind his ear. "I do."

"Why?"

"It was the most innocent I ever felt in my life," he said.

He unfastened his seatbelt and put his hand on the door handle. "I don't see the point of getting into it."

They were uncomfortably quiet for the rest of the ride.

When they parked, he unfastened his seatbelt and looked at her. *Is that really the same person? She looks so... weak.*

"You've heard the story," he said, "about the Christian who hid in a cave and found a lion?" He averted his gaze from her and stared at the steering wheel. "How there was a sliver in its paw and he took it out and the lion trotted out, and years later the man was captured and thrown into a coliseum up against a lion... it was that lion, and it licked him and everybody thought it was funny so they let him go. That's all Christianity means to me, just that really, it's not in the Bible, but I don't think any story's left such an imprint on me."

They sat there while Andrei waited for her to say something. She didn't and they went inside.

The walls were painted turquoise and covered with

photos the doctor had taken in 1960 of places like Machu Picchu, Persepolis, and Crete. Valeria spoke to the receptionist and Andrei sat down on a pleather couch beside a LEGO table covered in toys.

When Valeria sat next to him, Andrei lifted up the little mallet, ran it along the children's xylophone, and played a few bars from Bach's "Jesus, mein Freude." "I don't pray," Andrei said. "Maybe I have a few times... I did when my Dad lost his leg. I was always wishing for something. Why do you do it?"

"Because I feel guilty," Valeria replied, "because I feel scared."

"I don't think you should apologize for..." Andrei pulled back. They looked at each other and the conversation slipped away. Suddenly it didn't seem to matter to either of them.

"Valeria Ortiz," the doctor called out.

Valeria left Andrei.

Andrei clicked his heels together, then took out his phone to write out a message to his mother. After rewriting a few different messages, he decided to call her.

"Andrei? Everything ok?

"Yes, Mom."

"What's wrong?"

"I had an accident in school today—"

"Are you alright?"

"No, I accidentally stepped on a girl's glasses."

"Whose glasses?"

"Valeria Ortiz."

"The mayor's daughter?"

"Yes," Andrei said.

"Andrei, how could you!"

"It was an accident, Mom," Andrei said. "And I took

43

her to the eye doctor."

"What?"

"That's where I am now," Andrei said. "I was going to use my debit card to cover the costs of—"

"No Andrei, that's ridiculous."

"I told her I'd pay."

"No, I get that, but I'll cover the costs. Just keep the receipt with you and I'll transfer money to your account later."

"Mom, it's my fault."

"Oh, Andrei. You're being silly. Now, is there anything else you want to tell me?"

"I don't think so."

"Well, I found a broken-down pizza box in the garage. I thought I made it very clear. I will not allow you or your father to bring Berlusconi's Pizza into the house because it is unhealthy, disgusting, and makes the house stink. Your father knows this and now so do you. I also know that you used your allowance money to pay for your father's pizza. I'm not mad at you, but you will not pay for your father's bad health decisions."

"I don't think that Dad intended for me to—"

"Andrei, I know you're eighteen but you don't have a job, sweetheart. I think that it hurts your father more than you think when you try to cover for him like that."

"I hurt Dad's feelings?"

"I didn't mean that, honey. We'll talk later!"

When the eye doctor informed them that it would take a week, Valeria fell again into despair.

"I'll be your eyes," Andrei said, thinking he had made a funny joke. He recollected himself and said seriously, "I can pick you up and take you home every day this week. If you need to go anywhere, I'll take you."

After repeated insistence, Valeria agreed, and it occurred to her that this was the most pleasant and unexpected thing to happen to her thus far in the semester.

She lived far away. Andrei had to drive half an hour on the highway before exiting onto a country road that ran along forest and farmland. Despite her vision, she was familiar enough with the landscape that she could give him directions. They had gladly left behind their somber conversation and found shelter behind the music of the radio and the vibration of green and brown in the world around them.

Across a wire fence sloped western waves. The trees scattered about the meadow where goats and sheep meandered and grey dogs slept in shade. A ranch tiled with a Spanish roof rested in the distance with its back to the woods at the end of a winding dirt road. "That's your home?" Andrei asked as they drove closer.

Brick pillars supported the open wrought iron gates at the mouth of the road. As he turned, Andrei saw ornamental lions standing on their heels fixed to the gates, roaring with their tongues flicking out like snakes.

The summer wind blew back a cloud of dust onto Andrei's car. The gray dogs chased after him. He laughed. "I can't believe it."

She smiled and leaned her head against the window. "If you're not in a hurry, I'd love to show you around."

They parked beside a well by the ranch.

Valeria's mother, a brawny and cheerful person of Russian descent, came out the front door onto a white stone patio carrying a tray stacked with cheese, crackers, and a pitcher of lemonade. They met her at the table on the patio.

She set down her tray, hugged her daughter and then, much to his surprise, Andrei. "Andrei Goetz!" Janine Ortiz exclaimed. Though he could tell that she truly wanted him to feel welcome, Andrei doubted the sincerity of her delight, as if she were a child politely accepting a gift that she could not possibly want.

"Thank you for taking Valeria to the eye doctor," Janine said.

"I'm really sorry about that," Andrei said, "I promise that I'll pay for everything."

Janine laughed. "Oh don't worry about it. These things happen." Valeria sat on their table and poured Andrei a cup of lemonade. "What did you go with darling?"

"Not now," Valeria replied shyly. "How's Dad?"

"Sleeping like a baby, by the looks of it," Janine said, pointing to a hammock in a thicket of trees. "The dentist really put him under."

Andrei followed Janine's finger to the sun, and saw the mayor fast asleep. He was spread out with his face pressed against the side of the hammock. His long blond hair and bushy beard fanned out around him. His body was thick, muscular, and hairy, with a proud pot belly expanding and retracting as he slept.

Janine stood still and smiled at Andrei. "So, you must be getting into your college applications right now."

Andrei nodded uncomfortably. "I think I'm just going to go to Mizzou."

"Well..." Janine said, "I'm sure that your parents would like it if you stayed close to home."

Valeria's shoulders tightened toward her neck. She sipped her lemonade uncomfortably.

When Janine saw this, she turned to Andrei and said, "Why don't you stay for a while?"

"I was going to show him around," Valeria said, "if that's ok."

"That sounds like a great idea!" Janine said. "I'll be inside if you need anything."

She walked away back to the white ranch. Valeria remained quiet until Janine was out of sight.

"What do you think?

"You live in paradise," Andrei replied.

Valeria smiled at him, then coyly looked away. "That's nice of you to say," she said, "but I'd be much happier around people. It's lonely out here. At least in the city you'd hear cars passing by and see people...." her voice trailed off.

"You didn't miss the animals when you were gone?" Andrei asked.

"Not the goats or the sheep," she said, "just the horses."

"I still think that's amazing."

Valeria clicked her heels together. "Would you like to see them?"

She led Andrei past the well to a little white building by the corral. A bur oak stood between them.

Valeria rested a hand on the tree and smiled back at Andrei. "I climbed this tree when I was a kid and fell off and broke my ankle." She took a step forward toward the shadowy entrance of the barn.

In the glitter of the day he felt unsettled and followed after Valeria feeling as if he was being watched, as if he had something to feel ashamed of. Her airy passage through the world seemed ghostly. Andrei had always seen something eerie in the depiction of angels.

47

He did not take his eyes off of Valeria.

For some reason, Andrei felt like if he only took his eyes off of her for a moment she would vanish forever.

"Do you ever go into the woods?" Andrei asked.

"No," Valeria said, stopping, "why do you ask?"

"No reason," Andrei replied.

"I can't stand it at all," she said. "The woods here creep me out. You can't go without getting stung by thorns or getting bitten by a tick. I haven't gone since I was a kid. I had a friend who was very adventurous and we never saw anything good in there..." Valeria's footsteps hastened onward to the entrance of the stable.

Andrei felt very small as he stepped inside. He felt almost as if he was walking into church.

The hay crunched under their footsteps. The ceiling, he felt, was unreasonably tall.

"This is Canción," she said, and she put her hand on the forehead of a quiet chestnut mare that inched its snout closer to her. "You can touch her, if you want."

Andrei stroked a white streak of hair running between the mare's eyes. "Do horses have personalities?"

"Of course," Valeria said, and her hand brushed Andrei's. "Why wouldn't they?"

"The word personality would seem too..." Andrei stammered as he looked into the horse's eye.

"The more I've gotten to know any mammal the more I've felt like they were like us," Valeria said. The horse winnied and shook her head. "What's getting into you?" she asked gently.

"Does she not like me?"

Valeria shook her head. "It's ok," she said, stroking her head.

He looked down at the hay. He was bothered by

an unfamiliar odor, unsure if it was the horse or something else in the barn. *I feel so off,* Andrei thought. *It's like I'm in some kind of dream.*

"Valeria, I'm kind of thirsty. Do you mind if I grab a drink of..."

The horse backed onto its hind legs and sounded off in fear.

"Who are you, trespasser?" a man bellowed.

Valeria's father stood at the entrance of the stable wearing a white bathrobe emblazoned with his initials, "C.O." The curls of his unruly beard and wild blond hair fanned out into a monstrous mane. The glossy green eyes Valeria had inherited stung Andrei. Though the mayor's muscles were strong, haggard and wrinkled skin hung from his cheeks and arms.

"This is Andrei," Valeria said, laughing. "He's my friend."

"What shadow have you brought to my house?" the mayor asked.

"Cliff!" Janine Ortiz said, chasing after him. "He's delirious, don't mind him!"

The mayor shook his head furiously. "You scheme to take away my family, my home, my town, and drag it into the darkness?"

Janine grabbed his hand. "Come on Cliff, it's time to go back inside."

"Hands off of me, woman!" the mayor shouted, frightening the horses who neighed in terror. He pointed a finger at Andrei and staggered toward him. "Backpedal, retreat, scurry back into the blackness that bore you. You, wicked womanizer, I hear you every night as the wind, whispering into the heart of my daughter, corrupting her heart with your temptations, wicked,

49

wicked, wicked!"

Valeria and Janine screeched and the horses threw themselves about the stable walls.

Andrei's knees shook as the mayor drove him into a corner. His shadow seemed to stretch across the wall at a slant, towering over Andrei. The mayor took strong, brutish steps, and he stared furiously.

"You!" he shouted, drooling. His steps slowed and Andrei spread out his arms submissively.

"Oh!" the mayor moaned. He stumbled and fell. He curled up and bellowed as if he had been wounded. "I am a steward!" Then, silenced, his eyes trailed across the room, fixated. "Come," he whispered to something as his wife drew closer behind him. "What are you?" he asked gently, reaching out. "Shhhh…"

Janine, who was strong, grabbed him in a nelson hold. His eyes seemed to pop out of his head and he whimpered, desperately longing for that imaginary thing floating before him. "Cliff, shut up!" Janine said, yanking him backward. He writhed and struggled to break free.

"Leave me!"

Janine shrieked more furiously than Cliff, "Shut up!" Janine shook him. "Shut up!" She pressed him against a haystack. "Cliff! You're scaring the children!"

The mayor took deep breaths, relaxing into the hay.

Janine stroked his cheeks and he shut his eyes. She kissed him on the forehead, then looked at the children and feigned a smile.

"Kids, are you alright?"

"Yes," Andrei said and he turned to Valeria who was catching her breath.

"That was spooky!" Janine said, and she faked a

hearty laugh. "Andrei, would you mind helping me take him back to bed?"

"To bed?" Andrei asked, surprised. "Of course." He took a step closer to the mayor and just before he could touch him, the mayor's eyelids opened and he gasped for air.

Then the mayor's head fell limp as he snored.

Seeing how pale Andrei had become, Valeria intervened. "Andrei, I'll help my mom. Just... catch your breath."

THREE

Jonah Lipshitz had once wanted to be a great poet. He loved the wilderness and free-climbing. Deidra and Jonah met by chance at a hostel in Budapest and he was intrigued enough to look her up again when he was driving through Missouri.

The day Deidra found out that she was pregnant, he buried his ambitions and vowed to become a perfect father. At the bottom of his heart he believed this when he left suddenly, without a word, and moved back in with his parents in Rhode Island. Because he had left them in such states of ambiguity for the early years, Mary had her mother's last name. He returned to school and by Mary's third birthday had become a CPA.

This selfless sacrifice of his freedom had in fact left Deidra more alone and unsupported than if he had become a Boone County sandwich delivery man. They married, much to Deidra's surprise, after he had returned to them and secured a job.

Mary adored Jonah—once they were finally living together he lived for her. He knew everything that her heart desired. He took Mary to the park, taught her how to ride a bicycle, read to her every night, and when she became a pre-teen introduced her to his favorite musicians and films, shaping her tastes and passions.

But one day, to Deidra and Mary's complete surprise, he announced that he was leaving them to join the Israeli Self-Defense Forces, and, despite the weeping and pleading from his wife and child, departed the same day for Tel Aviv.

Once there, he was declared ineligible for service due to his age. Devastated, he visited a cousin who barely offered an ear before showing him the brilliant designs to an edgy guitar pedal.

The design and purpose astounded Jonah. Together they founded a successful company. Soon, Jonah abandoned book-keeping altogether and took to sales. He travelled across the Baltic States and elsewhere where jazz and metal musicians would marvel at his wares.

Entering his unpredicted prime, he reconciled with the Sarkisians through sheer charisma alone. Mary spoke with him every day on the phone as if nothing had happened. Deidra offered to buy tickets to go see him, but he quickly discouraged this. In truth, he had just taken in a mistress, a French teacher from Jordan, and he was captivated by his private world with her. "Mary wouldn't get the whole Israel thing because she's not a Jew or even a Christian," he said to Deidra on the phone, unaware that Mary was on the line.

This deeply wounded her, but Mary believed that one day he would make things right. She even believed that there was something she could do to make him come around. Mary asked her mother to find her some way to prove her Jewishness, and Deidra found a Reform temple in the community that welcomed her in its classes.

Mary learned how to read and write in Hebrew, and, when finally she would have her own Bat Mitzvah, her father was ecstatic. Both sides of the family were to come, and Mary counted the days until her father would arrive.

Then, quite unexpectedly, Jonah's cousin was hit in

a motorcycle accident, just before their biggest convention of the year in London. In the hospital, Jonah sat by his side, and his delirious cousin asked him to go to the convention and do what was best for the product.

Jonah tried to reason with him, but his cousin entered an incoherent monologue about Alexander the Great, Kurt Cobain, and the need for men to pursue greatness. Then his cousin said, "Do you really love them more than your future?" A question which shook Jonah and made him feel pathetic.

That night, he called Deidra and explained that this Reform temple wasn't truly Jewish enough by his standards, a "misunderstanding" Deidra thought could be cleared up by a call from the Rabbi, who was an adjunct professor at Washington University in St. Louis. Rabbi Isenberg attempted to reason with Jonah, explaining how hard Mary had worked and how dedicated she had been to their community. Eventually she passed the phone back to Deidra and said, "Sorry." Deidra wept as she pleaded with her husband. Mary sat frozen in a chair in Rabbi Isenberg's office. She felt like she was being peeled like an apple. A great numbness pervaded her body. Shattered, Mary refused to follow through with her Bat Mitzvah, and fled from God and tradition.

Deep down, Mary still hoped that one day her father would fix everything.

Mary could not forget the feeling from earlier in the day when Mr. Miet had sent her with Valeria to Sister Bernadette's office. The golden hue of one summer evening had caught her. They had spoken more in Mr. Miet's classroom after Valeria's presentation than they had all year. A sense of betrayal that stung her so deeply had been substituted with an overwhelming melancholy. She wished she could return to the summer of 2016. Though she tried to tell herself that it was over, Mary could not soothe the cries inside that demanded that Valeria be her friend again, that Valeria change, that the world return to the way it was before.

So, after her horrible school day, something sang in her heart as she saw several packages on her porch sent from her father across the sea. She opened them outside on that miserably hot day, and much to her disappointment found boxes of musical equipment and promotional materials.

Certain that this was a gift, but unsure of what it meant, she called her father on the phone.

Jonah was in the harbor on a yacht with his cohort and a group of Albanian models. Mary's voice sobered him up.

"Hi Pumpkin," he said. "I'm trying to get some sleep, what's up?"

"I got a few packages from you today," Mary replied. "Can you explain why?"

"I, uh, thought it was time to let you in on the family business. I wanted to give you the chance to do some promotion for us stateside, you know—"

"Dad?" She had heard voices around his father. "Why didn't you call me before—"

"You can really be a teenager sometimes," Jonah sighed. "Can we talk tomorrow morning your time? You know, when it's not before the crack of dawn, you know, when grown-ups aren't trying to sleep?"

"I'm… sorry Dad." Mary hung up the phone. Mary tried to hate him but instead she felt miserable, wishing that she had something in her heart that would make her father love her. Her inner chatter went quiet and she took the boxes inside carefully.

She went upstairs into the darkness of her room to put on one of her father's records on her father's record player. She lay on her bed listening to Mozart's "Requiem" on her father's speakers. "What a horrible night," she said, "to have a curse," quoting her father's favorite line from his least favorite video game.

Mary couldn't use her desk. It was covered in a great LEGO play set of Ancient Egypt she had built with her father years before he left and she never touched it, not once.

Mary felt shame in the savagery of her wailing. *What a disgrace,* she thought, *that my crying sounds like a mountain lion.* Her mother was sleeping with Andrei. *Was Valeria going to start sleeping with him too?* She was so desperate that she almost believed that the Devil himself would appear to wipe the tears from her cheeks.

Some day soon, she thought to herself, *I'll be gone.* She flipped through a thick catalogue of colleges that she kept by her bedside.

I have to study. I have to get ready.

The garage door opened.

She washed her face in the sink. With the lights off, she was a gray woman in a pale, dusty mirror. *She's not a girl like me.* Mary dried her face. *Soon life will pick up its pace. I'll find my place someday soon.*

"Honey, I'm having a student in ten minutes," Deidra called up the stairs. "Can you turn the music down? Don't you have Krav Maga tonight?"

Mary turned off the music and put her SAT books into her backpack. Her mother saw her as she walked down the stairs. "You didn't have to cut the music...

What are all these boxes here for?"

Mary stopped at the doorway and looked back at her mother. She feigned a smile. Her eyes were still red and swollen from her tears. "Dad sent me a stupid gift is all," she said, and she left.

~ ~ ~

After she crossed the gazebo and began the wretched journey down Calhoun Street on the way to Jason's, she was cat-called by a group of Neo-Nazis who jeered at her from a garage that was decorated with swastikas and ss equipment replicas. One of the men lewdly shook a pistol in front of his crotch and laughed.

They lost interest once they saw another woman walking down the sidewalk, a lady wearing a strange giant cap that dropped something like a mosquito net around her face and a dirty garden dress like from *Gone With the Wind*. "Annabelle, Annabelle!" They shouted, but the lady didn't seem to react. She carried a large basket filled with old dolls and toys. Something about the sight of this lady with these lazy-eyed dolls made Mary sick, the way she felt when she saw an elderly person stumble.

Mary couldn't catch the details of her face, but she was certain that this person was beautiful. Her figure was full in a way that intrigued Mary and yet her destitution and costumery made her seem so pure and untouchable.

Any desire that flickered in her subconscious was extinguished by a sense of repulsion.

Mary's hands were sweating.

The closer they came to each other the quieter the

world fell and the louder her pulse sounded.

She was certain that this lady would say something to her.

Mary tried to focus on the pavement.

How can it take so long to make it past one block?

The temptation to catch one complete look overtook her. The lady's dress was dirty and yet it seemed so smooth.

Mary wanted to see this woman's eyes. She wanted to know what it would mean to be caught in this woman's perception.

What if... What if...

The woman stopped within a few paces of Mary. Perhaps if the Neo-Nazis had not been jeering, Mary might have stopped as well. Instead she continued forward, now trying to pretend like she was oblivious to this stranger.

The woman turned her gaze to look at Mary as she passed by.

Mary shuddered.

There was no pleasure in this connection. Mary felt disgusted with herself.

Once she crossed the intersection she swore never to walk down that street again.

The aluminum cans reflected the sunlight all across Jason's front lawn. Dave sat on the front porch smoking a swisher. "Hey Mary, what's going on?!"

"Nothing much Dave," she said, walking by him.

"Hey," he chuckled, "isn't it past your bedtime?" He laughed and stomped his feet on the steps.

Jason was feeding his fish in his bedroom. He had left the TV on in the living room at a high volume. "What's wrong?" he said, surprised at seeing her come into his room. Then quickly he frowned, "Don't you know how to knock?"

"Do you want to hang out for a bit?" she asked. The red flakes drifted down on the ruined city of the fish tank like fire in slow motion. "I've had a bad day."

"It's not my problem," he said, and then he bit his lip. "I'm watching a movie right now, but you're welcome to sit on the couch."

"What are you watching?" Mary asked, but she knew from the sound of it that it was the *Chicken Little* movie. Jason rolled his eyes and in a moment she could see his face fluctuate from embarrassment to anger.

"Hey," Dave called out from outside, "you know what we could play?"

~ ~ ~

The world, being of one language, passed to the plain where it burned the brick and built the tower, and it was not lightning from above that brought it down, but rather because the world itself was confounded into several tongues. Brick by brick was looted until the gate to God collapsed like thunder.

"Jenga!" Dave shouted, and he fell onto his back like a turtle and wiggled his arms, laughing. Mary stood with a brick in her hand over the fallen Jenga tower, amazed by how much Dave was enjoying himself. Jason seemed surprisingly at ease and he happily started to rebuild the tower. Mary sat down on her calves and assisted him. She grinned at Jason and he turned his gaze to the table, deftly avoiding her fingers.

Jason had never sought love, except maybe once when he fell in love at first sight with a girl who worked at Sonic, but strangers fell for him like autumn leaves. Back when he was social, back when he still played live music, he saw people throw themselves at him, and for the most part this drove him away.

That girl from Sonic had come from the north and her beauty stood apart from her like a shadow. Of course he could have driven Mary away, though she bore a striking resemblance to that girl, but he couldn't see in Mary that separate beauty. One look from Mary and the city still stood, as did the republic.

Again, Mary clumsily toppled the tower.

No, Jason thought, *she looks like her, but she lacks the beauty that made me weak at my knees. A man never finds that beauty twice.* Still, it made him happy to see Mary. Having renounced a role in the world, he found some satisfaction in meaning something to Mary.

If Jason had a dream, it was that one day Mary would meet her, by chance on some flight to Singapore, when Mary had become somebody, and she would take Mary's drink order. That would be their only interaction, but to the earth alone, and not to another soul, it would be known that he linked them together.

"Again, Mary?" Dave asked. "I'm going to start calling you Butterfingers from now on!" Dave checked his phone and stood up. "I've got to go to work. I, uh, picked up another shift at Berlusconi's…"

"Worst pizza in town," Jason said.

"Yeah, but at least they don't employ illegals," Dave replied. "And on that note, don't go doing anything illegal, you two!"

"I'm of age," Mary said.

"Trust me, one day I'll see him on the news because of you!" Dave giggled and slapped Mary on the shoulder. "I'm kidding!"

Jason replied forcefully. "Don't you ever touch her again."

Dave raised his hands and grimaced. "Gee ref, I didn't touch the ball," he said, and he laughed again.

"Yeah, yeah, get out of here asshole," Jason said, and he put away the Jenga pieces into the box.

Once Dave had left, Jason swallowed and said, "Why did you come here today?"

"I wanted to see you."

He shook his head. "Isn't this way too weird? It feels criminal just to see you in my house."

"But it's not," Mary replied. "The only illegal thing you do is buy me cigarettes. It wouldn't even be illegal for us to have sex."

"You're the only teenager that comes here. Why?"

"Because you're my boyfriend."

"I'm not," he said. "Stop saying that I am."

"Well what do you want me to say?" Mary asked. "My life sucks. I don't have any friends. I actually enjoy spending time with you."

"Your life doesn't suck," Jason replied. "You actually have a future."

"You don't?"

"No."

Mary thought for a second. "Why do you think that?"

Jason sighed. "I live off of a trust fund that I have zero control over. Five hundred dollars come in every month and I spend it on booze, fast food, and a Brazzers subscription. Don't ask me why I'm not obese. My Xanax prescription is paid for from a separate fund that my parents set up for me that will cover my health care expenses until the day I die. I'm not capable of holding a job, I am too anxious to go to college, and I have panic attacks if I'm outside the house for more than a few hours." He shook his hands in the air. "Me and some fish! That's what my life is."

"I think you'll make a comeback," Mary said.

"You think so?" he replied sarcastically and pulled out a cigarette. "If I make a comeback, you're saying that I've been somewhere."

"Haven't you?"

He shrugged and lit the cigarette. "I had a good show in St. Louis," he said. "But I mainly played house shows with my friends. I never wrote a remarkable love song and I never recorded an EP. I played one solid show in St. Louis."

"Will you play a song for me?" Mary asked.

"Fat chance," he said. "I haven't played my guitar all year."

"Please, it would mean the world to me."

"My problems are small and so are yours, kid," he said. "Think of all the starving kids in India. You've got parents, a..." and he fell quiet, hearing Mary cry. She had buried her face into her sleeves and fell onto the couch.

"Don't talk to me about my mom," she said, and she erupted in ugly moans. Jason had forgotten the savagery of another person's crying. As Mary flailed in misery before him, something stirred inside, and he rushed to his room to pick up his guitar.

He returned under the doorway, shut his eyes, and played from his heart, unknowing what song would come out. One chord stumbled after another, until:

Should Old Acquaintance be forgot,
and never thought upon?
The flames of Love extinguished,
and fully past and gone:
Has your sweet Heart grown so cold,
in that loving Breast of thine
that you can never once reflect
On old lang syne?

The crying stopped. She stared up at him pathetically, and in the condescension that gripped his heart he felt he held a responsibility for this girl's welfare. She wiped the tears from her face and said, "What is this, New Year's?" Jason shook his head and set down his guitar. "Seriously, Jason. That was so cute what you just did."

Jason sat down in the armchair. "Cute."

"You looked really cool," Mary said. "I'm not being sarcastic."

He rubbed his forehead with the back of his fist. "Yeah…" he looked out the window at the setting sun. "Not to kick you out, but you should get home before it's dark."

Mary sat up and recomposed herself. "Yeah, my mom… I should get back."

"Do you want me to walk you as far as the park?" Jason asked.

She shook her head. "I'm good Jason. I really am."

He shrugged and slunk back into his chair. "Careful then…"

Mary slunk her backpack over her shoulder. She hesitated. "I wouldn't mind…"

She did feel safe walking beside him. He was quiet

along the way and noticeably awkward. Jason kept several feet between himself and Mary.

She tried making conversation and brought up the strange woman with the basket of dolls.

"Oh, Annabelle," Jason said.

"Who is she?"

"I don't know. She's just some crazy lady. Dave went to school with her. You could ask him next time you see him."

The cheap old gazebo had never seemed more beautiful, or perhaps ethereal, to Mary. The circle of cicada sounds rung and the sun flared on the horizon. "Well, best of luck Mary," Jason said. He turned around. "Stick to your guns."

When he walked away, Mary muttered, "Seriously, not even a hug?" to which he didn't reply.

~   ~   ~

Deidra sat on the front porch sipping a glass of red wine. She was looking up at a military plane streak across the purple sky.

"Welcome back home," she said. "I called your father and told him that he was a jerk." Mary sat beside her mother and tried to ignore everything she knew about her. "We've let you down," Deidra said.

"Don't say that mom," Mary replied.

"I wish that I could turn back time—"

"Please," Mary interjected, "I don't want to hear any of that tonight."

Deidra kissed Mary on the cheek. "Thank you."

Fireflies emerged across the neighborhood as they always had. When Mary had been little, Jonah and

Deidra helped her catch fireflies in jars and would release them back into the dark once Mary had been put
to bed. Seeing the fireflies float around the bushes and
trees made Mary feel love for her mother and father. In
this love she felt that at least for the moment she could
forgive them for anything.

When they returned inside, Deidra prepared a banana split. They shared it in the kitchen and listened to
a Joni Mitchell record.

"It's so funny. I can't believe how quickly time has
passed, how quickly you've grown. You've matured.
You've become so beautiful. But you've always had that
intensity in your eyes, like there are gunshots going off
and you're unfazed." She dug her spoon into the ice
cream. "I don't know where you got that determination
from." Mary looked at her mother wide-eyed, unsure
why she was bringing this up. "Do you remember when
I bought you that little cedar chest when you were a
kid?"

Mary shook her head. "I don't know what you're
talking about."

"When you were little, I bought a little chest from
an Amish trading post and I gave it to you. I told you
that I would never look inside. I read in a book that it
was a way to teach children about privacy. I'm sure it's
here somewhere… anyway, the point is, soon enough
you'll be a legal adult. Whatever you do and whatever
you choose to keep to yourself is your business. Some
would call me irresponsible for covering for you when
you cut class, but I know you well enough to know that
you must have your reasons, and I know better than to
pry. I just look at you and I know you can take care of
yourself. You're your own person. And I guess that's the

thing. A lot of times it's really hard for me to remember that I'm a person separate from being your mother, and the truth is that makes me struggle. I liked the idea of Ho-Tah Eh-Rey coming to stay with us because—"

The phone rang. Deidra answered. "Hello?" She listened for a bit, rolled her eyes, said, "Yeah, yeah, very funny," and hung up. She sat back down. "I'm pretty sure that moon-faced kid tried to prank call us again."

"Toby?" Mary asked.

"Would you feel like it was invasive if Ho-tah Eh-Rey moved in?" Deidra asked. "This is your home. I don't want you to feel like there's a stranger here."

"It's fine," Mary said. "If he's your friend, then—" The phone rang.

Deidra shook her head. "If it's him again I swear." She answered the phone. "Hello?" She listened again, but this time something noticeably struck her. Deidra glanced at Mary and her jaw dropped. "Go to hell!" she shouted and she ended the call.

"Mom?"

Deidra set the phone down on the table and turned nervously to Mary. "Didn't you bring in the mail?"

Mary shook her head. "I opened the packages."

Deidra marched past her daughter. She stepped outside and checked the mailbox. Mary followed her to the porch, hugging the side of the entrance nervously. Her mother removed a red envelope. Deidra dug a fingernail in a corner under the fold and used it like a letter-opener.

She felt inside expecting a letter but instead found the key to her home.

The banana split melted as they waited for the police to come.

By the time the locksmith had left, the banana fell like a sinking ship into the puddle of vanilla ice cream. A fly perched on the bowl's edge. The banana sank and hit the bottom of the bowl.

Deidra took the bowl and the fly flew off. She dumped its contents into the trash. The ice cream trickled down rotten meat and produce. There were maggots at the bottom of the bag.

As Mary lay in her bed she found herself trembling, even though she had assured her mother that she was okay. She was parched and her eyes were glazed. Without hearing a word or thought she could feel whispers over her dry heart.

Deidra sat at the kitchen table by herself after having shuttered the kitchen windows. She made a call on her cell phone.

"I need you."

FOUR

*I*t must be traumatic for a god to feel pain, something like the first time a child discovers shame. After the drama in the Garden, Adam and Eve felt shame in their nakedness, covering themselves in leaves or ferns. Missouri, of course, is a place where it is widely unquestioned that the acquisition of knowledge would prompt humanity to hide its genitals, and if, as the Mormons claim, the Garden of Eden was in fact in Jackson County, then shame was the first byproduct of a Missouri education.

They did not cover their nakedness because the apple taught them that clothes were good and nudity bad, but rather because in their weakness and humiliation this was their basic attempt to put a veil between themselves and the world. The apple may be strongly correlated to this re-action, but it would be a presumption to cite the apple as causation; after all, in light of the same truth, Lucifer (the second strongest being in the Bible) and his hundred react-ed with a coup d'etat. If Adam and Eve had enough power to defeat the seraphim guarding the gate to Eden, would the story have gone differently? Had they been armed with God-killing thunderbolts as Zeus was by the cyclops in the war against his father, would Genesis have concluded in deicide?

The King of Bavaria was born to wealth and power, and he refused to feel shame. Shame is a barrier that sepa-rates humans from greatness and when somebody of great strength forgets shame then they can make reality into a fairy tale. The best and most innocent people believe in *fairy tales, even when we cannot, and the King of Bavaria sponsored the birth of many works of music, art, and theatre that are widely celebrated each year and have given employment to thousands upon thousands of artists. In my opinion, this is the most productive and ethical use of power: converting this savage world of shame into a place we can only now shamelessly believe in.*

~ ~ ~

Andrei looked out the dirty window and saw a police car turn into the parking lot. A roly-poly police officer squeezed out and walked strenuously up the hill to school. Andrei imagined him falling over and rolling down the hills like a cartoon character.

His German teacher had caught him looking off and he shot his gaze back to her. She stood at the front of class reading from the teacher's textbook as the other students repeated her words. Andrei saw her face crease slightly as she looked backed down and he felt that he had wounded her.

Ms. Gale was the only teacher at St. Sebastian's that Andrei cared about; when pushed into a corner by adults demanding to know his career path, he answered that he would teach German. To some extent he felt disgusted by himself for over-preparing because it reminded him of how he over-prepared for piano with Deidra Sarkisian. Suffocating in shame, he rejoined the choral repetition of the lesson's vocabulary, and, when Ms. Gale's eyes fell again upon him, he feigned enthusiasm.

Her ashen hair was long and curly, her features narrow and sharp. A round pair of spectacles slid down the bridge of her nose, and whenever she turned the page she would push them back up.

When class let out, Ms. Gale called for Andrei to stay. "I've read your homework," she said. "I was really impressed—you really worked hard this summer. Ideally I'd switch you to German Four, but since we're alternating every year now... I hate to say it but you're stuck."

"That's okay," Andrei said. "I'm not really comfortable with this stuff yet."

"Well," Ms. Gale smiled, "there's another student like you."

"Who?" Andrei said, and she laughed at his incredulity.

"Do you remember Joseph Kruger?" she asked.

"Didn't he transfer?"

"He got very sick unfortunately, but he's still a student here. He just does school work remotely. Technically, he's in this class," Ms. Gale said, "and he's wonderful. I think you guys should do a project together."

"Umm... that would be fine."

"I promise you won't regret it. So I'll put you two in touch then?"

"Sure," Andrei replied, and he tried to smile.

"Seriously, you'll love him," she said. "I wouldn't even bring it up if I didn't feel that you guys would take each other to the next level." He waited for a moment to see if there was anything else. "Alright!" This time Ms. Gale's smile was false and this social cue embarrassed Andrei. He left hurriedly and cursed himself.

Andrei walked through the Gothic corridors decorated with silver and green ribbons and banners, past the dusty trophy cabinets to his locker. *Oh fuck me,* he thought, *and fuck these people too.*

He loathed group work above all else. It was to him a giant waste of time and an exercise in self-censorship. Andrei had no interest in Joseph Kruger, a boy he remembered only because freshman year he had a seizure during Thursday mass as an altar boy. *This has nothing to do with me. Some adults felt the need to intervene and give a sick boy a friend.*

Andrei reached his locker, surprised to find a pink sticky note:

Dugout. Lunchtime.

~　~　~

Andrei waited outside the double-doors of the auditorium as the students flooded in. His arms were crossed and he rested against the wall on one leg.

Toby leapt out and charged at Andrei with a closed fist. "Bump it dude," he said. Andrei politely tapped his fist. "What are you waiting for?" he asked.

"Valeria," Andrei replied.

"Dude, you didn't hear this from me," Toby leaned in, "but I overheard some girls say that Valeria used the largest size of tampon available." Toby nodded, as if he were affirming some response from Andrei. "She must have been preggers," Toby whispered. "I mean seriously. What else could it have been? Who leaves to spend a year with their aunt in Kansas City?"

Andrei saw Valeria approach like a suitcase on a baggage carousel. "Shut up, Toby." Andrei called out her name. She smiled and stepped toward them.

"What's going on, V?" Toby asked.

Valeria blinked, then smiled. "How are you, Toby?"

"Never been better," Toby replied. "I'm on a cleanse."

"A juice cleanse?" Valeria asked.

"Not exactly," Toby said. "Tang and the liquid food they give to astronauts in NASA."

Her eyebrows rose up. "Uh... are you trying to lose weight or—"

"Just between you and me, mademoiselle," Toby began, making her blush uncomfortably, "NASA's space project may be a lie, but their food program was very real. What do you think was keeping Old Man Rothschild alive past one hundred?"

"Astronaut food?" Valeria asked.

"She's a keeper!" Toby said, holding his belly from the bottom-most roll and laughing.

Ashamed, Andrei impulsively took Valeria's hand and said, "Come on." The moment his hand grabbed hers, his insides froze. Andrei looked at Valeria, whose face was still blushing, and he wanted to evaporate.

"Yes," she said, "let's take a seat."

A dim light rested on the stage. An old blue velvet curtain hung behind a podium adorned at its base by white feverfew daisies.

Toby followed from behind. Andrei sat at the edge of a row in the back to send Toby a signal, but Toby chose to sit on the other side of Valeria.

Mr. Messner, the vice principal, stood by a guest at the stage's footsteps. Mr. Messner wore eye-liner and topaz studs. His beard was cut close to his skin and oiled. He smiled merrily as he spoke with the guest and noticed a cue from a faculty member in the back. Seeing that the students were all seated, Mr. Messner approached the podium.

"Good morning students," Mr. Messner said, and a

light fell upon him. "Today, to remember the tragedy of Hiroshima, we welcome Dr. Nicholas Nakayama, a political scientist from Washington University in St. Louis, who is a renowned expert on nuclear defense policy, institutional and state collapse, and armageddon in human society and culture. Please welcome Dr. Nakayama."

This description humored the guest speaker, who ascended the steps to a polite applause. His long sideburns, shaggy head of hair, and hairy chest exposed by a couple loose buttons of his black shirt made him seem anything but professorial.

The professor shook Mr. Messner's hand and yanked on his own collar. "So, actually, this fabric is specially designed to be breathable in summer, but," he smiled, "what was I thinking wearing black?" Even though there was nothing explicitly funny in what he said, the aloof and relaxed manner in which he spoke provoked laughter from the faculty. "Thanks Mr. Messner. I can take it from here."

A white screen descended center-stage. "Alright, look at that," he said. "I love how we're building the anticipation, so…" He tapped on the microphone sending piercing reverberations out. "Sorry, I, uh, didn't think this was on. So Mr. Messner was basically right, I published some papers on nuclear war and the fall of institutions and societies, and, uh, a book recently about how the two could be related, and uh, right now I've got a grant to study at the University of Missouri, uh," he chuckled, "you can put two and two together on that one, ok, there we go, screen's ready."

"By the way," Dr. Nakayama said, "I'm an American scholar and I'm coming at this from a very American—

perhaps too American—point of view." The first image appeared on the screen, a lithographic depiction of the four horsemen of the apocalypse. "Let me start this off by saying that yes, somebody always claims that the sky's falling. There's a passage from the Book of Revelations: And I saw a white horse: and he that sat on him had a bow; and a crown was given unto him: and he went forth conquering, and to conquer. And there went out another horse that was red: and power was given to him that sat thereon to take peace from the earth, and that they should kill one another: and there was given unto him a great sword."

At this moment Andrei felt Valeria's knee bump against his. He sat still. *Is it ever really accidental?* From the corner of his eye, Valeria seemed to be fixated on the lecture.

"So Atilla's running around through Europe, or the Mongols, or Napoleon, and you point to the Book of Revelation and, everybody says, 'well that's it.' But of course that was never the end of things. Quick question, I want to see a show of hands here. Who thinks that before the invention of the nuclear bomb that humanity was capable of wiping itself out and the world out, isolated cases like Easter Island aside, I'm talking about humanity as a whole, hands go down I see... people get that nuclear war will mean the end, at least to civilization as we know it, and the assumption that people will avoid it is so strong that there is a whole school of thought centered around the idea that this fear is enough to keep us out of nuclear war, something more people believe in than climate change, that is to say nuclear deterrence. By the way, show of hands, who believes in climate change? Oooo... dear. Anyway..."

A black and white image of a girl holding a flower appeared on the screen. "Let's roll the clip."

The girl was in a field, counting as she plucked the petals from the leaves, "seven… eight…" when suddenly a nuclear bomb exploded. A Texan's voice said, "These are the stakes: to make a world in which all of God's children can live, or to go into the dark. We must either love each other, or we must die." Then another man's voice said, "Vote for President Johnson on November 3rd. The stakes are too high for you to stay home."

Dr. Nakayama coughed. "Can you imagine that they ran that on TV? I think that the candor makes us laugh. It's the editing, the intensity followed by that quick transition to a monotonous voice. This fate, scary enough to drive Americans to the voting booth, is precisely what we subjected Japanese children and civilians to in 1945. And it was precisely because we had subjected children and civilians to this in 1945 that we were afraid of it. It wasn't a hypothetical. We had it, the Russians had it, and it had weight because we saw what it did. Because of Hiroshima it was indisputable that humans would use it and we made them bigger, stronger, and in greater numbers not to be never used but to be used if, if, it was in our strategic interests. Some people will say that when you talk about Hiroshima, you talk about the victims, but I disagree. We should talk about how we as Americans justify it. Can anybody tell me why we dropped the bomb?"

He waited for a second. Toby threw his hand up and spoke up before Dr. Nakayama could call on him. "It would have been too costly," Toby said, "to ourselves and the Japanese, in terms of human life."

"Thank you for speaking up. I've heard it projected

that five hundred thousand U.S. soldiers would have died taking Tokyo Bay, not that I've ever seen a military document or primary source stating that. It seems to have originated in Halbersteim's biography of Truman, but there's no citations there, so we're not sure where he got the figure from. Churchill said a million, and I think it could have cost that many or more lives. Probably a lot more. But we're operating under an assumption here. It is undeniable that it would have taken a high number of casualties to force total surrender of the Japanese Empire, and it is from this perspective indisputable that the first bomb, in this cost-benefits analysis, was better than an amphibious landing. The assumption is that we're not challenging adherence to the Potsdam Declaration, we're not challenging the necessity for unconditional surrender. We know, for a fact, that the Japanese were willing to surrender if the Imperial Institution and a group of Class A war criminals had been guaranteed sovereignty, control, privilege, and power over Japan. And guess what, students, even with unconditional surrender, they got that. Unconditional surrender didn't change the fact that Japan would continue to have an Emperor and even though we tried and hanged some war criminals, class A war criminals continued to lead the so-called democratic country."

Black and white footage of Japanese people protesting took the screen. "These are the 1960 Anpo protests, when the Japanese legislature—the Diet—voted on the treaty that tied our military interest with theirs. This government of war criminals forcibly ejected anybody who would vote against the alliance with our support. We didn't drop the bomb for democracy. We didn't drop the bomb to save lives. Forget that nonsense! Yeah, we showed those Japanese for punching us in the nose in Pearl Harbor! Yeah we really knocked their teeth out! If any of you bozos want a piece of America we've got more missiles with your name on them!"

Dr. Nakayama waited, scanning the crowd. In his silence, images of the bedlam and destruction of Hiroshima flashed on the screen, each lasting less than a second. "The proliferation of nuclear missiles simply increases the scale by which a geography can be transformed into Hiroshima 1945. At this point, the Earth and the Sea could become Hiroshima. Hiroshima is more than about victims and an ethical dilemma, it was the ultimate self-revelation of what it means to bend morality by a consequence-driven equation. Somewhere, in your homes, in your classrooms, someone will methodically go through each point in my argument and conclude, pointing a finger at these ruins and burnt bodies, orphans and survivors, that this was justice, and it will always hinge on that consequentialist picture frame. But I promise you one thing, this kind of reasoning does not stop at Hiroshima, it will follow you everywhere you will go, and will drive all societies—as it always has—to collapse. We are however, past collapse, we are at extinction's door. Let any idiot die on a hill shouting, 'the atom bomb falling on Hiroshima was justified,' but it is the words of LBJ that must sound over it if we are to survive, 'These are the stakes: to make a world in which all of God's children can live, or to go into the dark. We must either love each other, or we must die."

~ ~ ~

Oh, Mary Sarkisian, Andrei thought, *what evil plot have you concocted today?* Andrei skipped lunch, bent on anticipating Mary in the baseball field. As he crossed campus, he passed the soccer field where a mix of boys and girls played. *What happy simpletons they are,* Andrei thought.

He could recognize some of these athletes from when he was getting ready for what would have been his first soccer practice, back in freshman year. Almost exactly three years ago, he had dressed himself in the locker room, ambivalent to the boasting around him. As they left that smelly den he had felt miserably closed off. He had put his cleats behind the gym on the grass while some of his would-be teammates ran off to the field.

"Hey," Jessi Lang had said, lying on the grass. She spoke in a tone that made Andrei feel that she was completely indifferent to him. She sat up. Her eyes were made-up in heavy black and her hair was dyed a vicious red. "Who are you?"

"I'm Andrei."

"I'm Jessi," she said and she sat up. "Want to go to the creek?"

"The creek?"

"Uh-huh," she said, "and see where it goes to."

"Why?"

"You're cute and all," Jessi said.

So of course Andrei had blown off practice.

Andrei could not make up his mind on whether or not he had been lucky. Passing by the soccer players he had never known, he could not help but feel contempt for the alternative futures he had avoided.

He had never been in the dugout and was hovering on the cement above it when he heard Mary's voice. "Just jump."

He reluctantly leapt down and landed gracefully.

Mary was leaning with her elbows resting up behind her, smoking a cigarette. Andrei eyed his grandfather's necklace. Mary raised her box of American Spirit Blacks. "Want one?"

"No, thank you," Andrei said. "Just the necklace."

"Tell me," Mary said grimly, "did you enjoy sleeping with my mother?"

"I don't want any trouble," Andrei said.

"What did you think?" Mary asked. "That you would make a mockery of my family and I wouldn't give you any trouble for it?"

Andrei shook his head. "I didn't mean to hurt you, Mary."

"Oh go to hell. We both know you got what you wanted, or are you going to say—"

"I won't," Andrei blurted out. "Tell me what you want."

Mary chucked her cigarette. "Quit coming to our house," Mary said cooly. "I don't want to see you at my house or around my mother ever again."

"Ok, but... won't that raise more eyebrows?"

Mary scowled. "You're afraid of getting caught. It's my mother who'd get branded. I'm sure you'd just get a high five."

"I do care about your mother," Andrei said, and Mary laughed at this. Humiliated, Andrei turned away to face the field. "Whatever you say then."

"Good," Mary said, "but how can I trust you?"

Andrei sighed. "Surely you've thought this through."

"I did. I've seen you with Valeria."

"You'd tell her?"

"No," Mary replied, "but Valeria said some damning things to me. Last year she texted me some horribly problematic things that you can't really get away with in our generation."

"You're serious?" Andrei asked. "You'd hurt her just to punish me?"

"You two are birds of a feather," Mary said. "It's not that you or Valeria did something wrong that causes your anxiety, it's that you care about what people find out. So what do you say?" she asked. "Don't you want your grandfather's necklace back?"

"Yes, I do."

Mary unfastened the chain and tossed it at his back. It stung him and rage overcame his shame. He bent over and picked it up, staring Mary down. "I'll go then," he said.

"Fuck off," Mary replied.

~ ~ ~

Andrei had passed much of the afternoon in the nurse's office. The nurse, who could see that Andrei was in distress, asked for his symptoms, and when Andrei said "nausea," the nurse told him to lie down on a cot in a dark room.

As the nurse shut the door, she asked Andrei if anything was troubling him. Somehow, Andrei felt that the nurse had caught onto his ruse. "It's ok," the nurse said. "Rest, and if you want to talk, I'm outside."

Andrei stared up at the ceiling not daring to doze

off for fear of seeing new apparitions in his sleep paralysis, but he wanted to forget himself.

Mary was right, he thought. He had humiliated her. He had threatened to bring shame upon her mother's name.

It was not a good thing.

He had his chain back. His affair with Deidra had been concluded in the deal. In some ways he saw that he was better off.

So why did he feel so unhappy? "Play it again," Deidra had said, weeping out of nowhere, "play it again." He repeated the musical phrase over and over until he realized that no amount of playing could stop her tears. He lifted his fingers from the white keys and turned to face her. As she cried beside him on the piano bench, Andrei realized that her tears had nothing to do with how he played. *She's in pain,* he realized.

Deidra had been a magical being to him. She had walked him through that door and made him feel so brilliant and kind. He had been a star in her eyes. He would have done anything to calm her.

Andrei embraced Deidra and when he met her cat-like eyes he kissed her.

Had it been so wrong?

Yes, Andrei thought, *yes, but only because I was stupid enough to get caught!* His blood seemed to sink like syrup. Mary had been right, he realized. He wasn't sorry for getting what he wanted. His private world had been discovered and this alone brought him pain.

The shame passed for a moment. He would stick to his word. The time would come to tell his father that he was quitting piano. He needed some excuse. With sadness in his heart he remembered his last recital when he played "Jesus Bleibet Meine Freude." The composition had felt like a love letter to his life. His heart felt as light as it had before his father's accident. He soared from grace with each note. As he shed a tear, Andrei found himself weightless. *Perhaps I am free after all,* he thought. *Perhaps I have been spared.*

So, Andrei fell asleep, and no visions haunted him. For the first time in a very long time, he slept peacefully, surrounded by the heart and mouth and deed and life. It was as if he had been caught in some reverent wedding ceremony, waiting for the bride to come out. He could taste the white cake cut on some elegant Mother's Day lunch at a purely white restaurant. Whatever it was, it remained his heart's repose, and the most chaste lust and sun in his eye.

He woke and remembered what it was like to do the backstroke as a child in the pool, staring up at the ceiling. The peace and pace of the music had stayed with him. Andrei felt like he could only have been asleep for a moment, but felt rejuvenated. He sat up and pushed the door open. The lights of the office were off, and the bright sunlight poured over Valeria, who sat nonchalantly with her back to the window, reading a book.

She looked up at Andrei and smiled. "What's wrong?" she asked.

"Nothing's wrong," Andrei said. "Why should something be wrong?"

Valeria shut her book and stood up. "You've been sleeping in the nurse's office all day. School's out."

"But the nurse?"

"Bathroom," Valeria said. "It's three-forty-five. School's out."

"And you're waiting for me?"

"You're my ride."

"Do you want to get ice cream?"

Valeria blushed. "Andrei, I'm lactose-intolerant."

"I'd like to go somewhere we can talk," Andrei said. "Would that be okay?"

"I'd like that," she said. "We could go down a trail I like."

~ ~ ~

"Bird on a Wire," by Leonard Cohen started to play when they reached a stoplight. After a few bars, Valeria asked if they could change it. Andrei asked why, because he loved it, and she quickly replied, "I don't want to listen to a dead man talk." He skipped it and a grumpiness filled the space between them. It lasted only as long as the stoplight.

The road ran up the steepest hill lined on the sides by endless trees. It seemed to jut into the sky, as if the car would fly off into the blue.

Pulling off an exit to a winery, Andrei drove by fields of grape vines. They parked close to a trailhead by a wooden railing that loomed over the Missouri River. They watched how the river snaked through the forested hills. Kayakers in the water were as small as ants.

"Do you think that this is the river that ran to the ocean in Kansas?" Valeria asked.

"What are you talking about?"

"Kansas used to be an ocean, you know?" Valeria said, and seeing that Andrei didn't know, she quietly added on, "a shallow one at that," and fell silent.

"I didn't know that," Andrei said.

"When I had my breakdown I wanted to go to the

ocean. I don't know why, but I just drove west, and I ran out of fuel before I reached Topeka. I got out of my car and walked onto the grassland and imagined myself up to my waist in sea water."

Andrei couldn't decide whether he thought this was beautiful or scary.

Choosing to follow a rusty train track into the woods instead of the park trail, Andrei and Valeria came into a ravine where wildflowers and dandelions flourished. He grabbed her hand. He appreciated how quiet they could be. They could hear the birds and felt the trees far to the edges of this clearing bend around them purposefully.

Valeria found a small booth abandoned on top of a knoll. Its windows had been knocked in and old railway controls rusted inside. Graffiti covered its concrete walls. Andrei followed behind her, intrigued by her sudden burst of energy. She took some photos of things that interested her and found a can of spray paint. Andrei stood by the booth checking for any signs of people. Valeria rattled the can and squatted. She sprayed it and found that it still had a considerable amount of paint inside.

Andrei studied her movements. In thick, confident strokes she drew something in Cyrillic, and when he asked what she was writing, she ignored him. "Isn't it funny that we were the only freshmen at prom that year?"

"It was ironic."

"You and Jessi weren't part of anybody's group though."

"Jessi and I went to dinner alone."

"You ever hear from her?" Valeria asked.

"No," Andrei said.

"Nobody knows if you guys broke up or anything like that," Valeria said. "It's one of the great mysteries of school." The can gave out as she drew a crown. She tossed it to the dirt and it rolled down the hill.

"We lasted a while," Andrei said. "I even visited her over spring break last semester. I don't know, once I got my SAT results in, Stanford really didn't seem like much of an option anymore. She gave up on me, I guess you could say."

Valeria nodded. "Do you want to squat in front of the wall? I'll take a good photo for you, for when you get on Tinder… are you eighteen yet?"

Andrei squatted down and posed. "I turned eighteen in July."

After she took his picture she posed with him in a selfie and told him to stay still. He asked why and she kissed his cheek.

She sat and rested with her knees bent along the ground. She took a photo of him again and he came toward her, resting his knuckles on the earth around her thighs.

Valeria lowered her phone and stared into his eyes. The more time he spent with her, the more he could pick emotion from her static voice. "It means Prince Andrei," she said, and he could sense melancholy in her tone, the way people sound when they reflect on somebody they have already mourned.

He leaned in to kiss her and they fell into the dirt.

"It's ok," Valeria said. Andrei undid the first button. As his hands passed to the second he looked into Valeria's eyes. A thick layer of pink spread across her nose and cheeks. He exposed her clavicle and found a necklace with a little jeweled egg unlike any he had ever seen.

"What's this?" He worked his way down her shirt.

"A Fabergé Egg," Valeria said. "It belonged to my great-grandmother on the Russian side. She was a countess…"

Andrei fit an open palm on her open chest, then pressed his ear to her heart. She ran her fingers through his hair.

He kissed the little stone and caressed her thighs. She dug his nails into his shoulders with each kiss. Her mouth moistened with the touch of his lips. Salivating, she dug a hand into his scalp and said his name between her moans, "… Andrei… oh Andrei." She stared up into the sky she had sworn was clear and saw the countless lines of mackerel clouds splitting before the yoke of the afternoon sun. "… Andrei," she repeated, the sound of her voice lost in her esophagus, desperate to be let out. Her long, polished fingernails dug into the back of Andrei's wrist and dragged down to his knuckles. Her fingers slid between the spaces between his fingers. She squeezed as she had when a piece of glass had been removed from her body.

She knocked Andrei onto his back, taking him by surprise with the affection and force of her kisses, seeking to release him. The fear of getting caught like a tongue to a lamppost in the dead of winter had dissolved in his warmth. She reciprocated his hunger and touch.

Ship-wrecked, he raised his head up and saw her smile on the other end of the train track, though he himself was stranded in the turn-style of her green eyes.

They sank deeper together and held themselves on the hot cement. It was scalding—had been scalding since they touched it—but they felt bound to it by an immense gravity. Sweat ran down their collarbones. A hawk circled above them as Andrei's eyelids fell.

"I wish I could fall asleep next to you," she said.

"Me too."

"I bet you sleep like an angel."

"Not at all," Andrei replied groggily. He hesitated. Thoughts of the black-oiled woman came to mind and Valeria felt him shiver. "I often have nightmares," Andrei murmured softly, "and wake up in the middle of the night and see things."

"Like demons?"

Andrei nodded his head slightly.

Valeria eyed him cautiously. "Do you hear laughter?" Valeria said sorrowfully.

"Laughter?" Andrei asked, slightly confused by Valeria's tone. "Not really. They say things to me, sometimes in German, but it's always like being visited at the hospital. The things I see are horrible, but I don't think that they're making fun of me.

"There's laughter in mine," Valeria said, "something horrible about how I'm untrustworthy, unfaithful, that I'll throw somebody under the bus one day, somebody who loves me more than anything... They said that I'd suck dry the person who loves me. That I'm a parasite... I must sound crazy."

"Of course not," Andrei replied. He tried to find some way to bridge their divide. She had identified some common ground and yet it felt so awkward and unrealistic. "Why would I think that?" But this question only seemed to sting her. "It's so creepy... I saw the scariest thing. I feel like my room's a different place because of it, even though it was just a dream... there was this woman just dripping in oil... or tar..."

The air became icy and the clouds consumed the sun. She pulled herself up and slipped on her shirt. Valeria walked off toward the river and stepped barefoot over the rocks and leaves.

"Wait!" He pulled his white t-shirt over his chest and slipped on his shoes. "Just wait for me." He hurried after her, half-afraid that she would jump off into the river.

She was standing still, though very frightened, behind a cypress tree that reached out past the ledge above the water. He grabbed her by the arm. "You're not a parasite," Andrei said. "If anything it's the world that's fed off of you."

Valeria turned around to face him but couldn't make eye contact. Her eyes were fixed on the Missouri River. "What if I broke down right now or tomorrow or next week? I don't want to get sent away." She was crying. "I don't want to be stuck at home as a... child forever, taking classes at community college alone... alone." She hugged him and they felt the warmth of each other's chests.

She buried her eyes into Andrei's shoulder.

Andrei was so confused. He lost himself in the glimmer of light on the river and saw the other shore.

~   ~   ~

"Dad, I think I need to take a break from piano lessons," Andrei said to his father in the garage. "At least until I finish taking the SAT." Henry Goetz was hunched over, chiseling at something.

"Uh-huh," Henry Goetz said. "How are they conflicting?"

"I just don't have the time."

Henry set down the wood block and turned around. "Well," Henry Goetz said, "that's not true, is it?"

"What?"

"I got a call from the mayor. He said that you and his daughter have started dating each other."

Andrei blushed. "I wouldn't call it that. I've been helping her out because I—"

"Broke her glasses by accident," Henry said. "Your mother told me. The mayor says he was under some pain medication after his dental surgery and that he might have spooked you. What was that about?"

"He just got angry and passed out."

"Son, the mayor wants to have us over for lunch on Friday. How serious are you and Valeria?"

"I have school Friday."

"Oh no, it's Back-to-School Night. You've got a half-day," Henry Goetz said. "She your girlfriend?"

"We've technically been on just one date."

"So then why are the parents meeting each other?"

"I don't know!" Andrei replied. "Did he say why?"

"He said we should all get to know each other better."

"Why?"

"Because you're taking out his daughter, that's why."

"But she's not my girlfriend," Andrei said. "We just get along."

"Good," Henry said. "So I can stay home, but you need to go."

"Why?"

"Because he's the mayor and you're taking out his daughter. It's part of the territory," Henry replied. "It's a good thing. Maybe he can get you a job."

"Why would the mayor give me a job?"

"What part about the, 'you're taking out the mayor's daughter,' thing are you not understanding, son? Imagine that you were the richest man in town and some teenage boy started taking your teenage daughter out. Wouldn't you want to meet him?"

"Ok," Andrei replied, "but I've only just started to think about her in this way."

"Will you let me talk?" Henry said. "He likes you, or at least the idea of you, a lot, and he doesn't want you to be scared of him. He just doesn't want you and his little girl to feel like you are star-crossed lovers."

"So I have to eat with him?" Andrei asked.

"He wanted us to join his family for lunch Friday afternoon. I'll lie and say I've got the stomach flu, but you still need to go."

"What about mom?" Andrei asked.

"Mom's got work," Henry said. "Andrei, you want to quit your piano lessons?"

"At least for until I take the S.A.T."

"Oh, so you have time for a girlfriend but not for studying?"

"Dad!"

"I'm just saying what your mother would say. I'm happy to see you with a friend, romantically or not. In my view you never had time to make any friends because of the goddamn piano. So I'm going to cover for you, but you have to go to that lunch."

"Are you sure?" Andrei asked, blown away by his strange fortune.

"Yes."

"Well, thank you."

"Now," Henry said, "why don't we go to celebrate white lies over a pizza?"

"Do you mind if we order Chinese instead?" Andrei asked, knowing that his father was alluding to Berlusconi's.

Henry frowned. "Why Chinese?"

"I'm in the mood for Chinese is all," Andrei said.

"Fine. We can order take-out."

~ ~ ~

The molten metal flowed into the mould. The weathered man's gray hair hung wildly down his naked shoulders. An old apron was fastened around his fat belly. When it hardened, the smith pounded the hot metal with a wooden mallet, grunting with each blow.

JR sat outside the forge on the dirt in the hot sun, drinking from a bottle of goat's milk. He wore a pair of sweatpants with his pot belly sticking out. His skin was soft and smooth. His muscles were strong. He had a devilish goatee and a long braided pony-tail resting on his shoulder.

A St. Bernard ran over to him. JR petted him lovingly as the dog licked his face. A little girl in a checkered blue dress hurried happily towards him. "JR!" she shouted, gleefully running after the dog. "When did you get here?"

JR smiled. "I've been here all day."

"What's Daddy making you?"

"What do you think?"

The girl thought for a moment. "A claymore?"

JR shook his head. "Nope." The St. Bernard lay next to him, panting intensely. He took a swig from the bottle.

"Well… some kind of sword."

"That's right," he said.

"What Ren Fair are you going to?" the girl asked.

"No Renaissance Fair."

"Then why do you need another sword?"

"It's a gift."

"For who?"

"Some kid who's about to grow up down in Missouri. I can't leave town without it."

That night JR sat at the table with Muzzy and the little girl. They had sweet rolls, ribs, and collared greens.

"Daddy," the girl said. "Can I say grace?"

"Of course darling," Muzzy answered.

JR, Muzzy, and the girl laid their hands on the table, grabbing each other's fists. The girl shut her eyes and recited the words from memory:

"Your blessings are many
Our Harvest is Plenty
Dear Stranger, Dear Stranger
We wait in your Manger
Whisper your task
from your sweet mask."

The men spoke in unison, "We're Waiting, still Waiting."

Once Muzzy had put his daughter to sleep, they smoked cigars together outside on the patio.

"When are you headed down?" Muzzy asked.

"As soon as you're finished," JR replied.

Muzzy puffed on the cigar. "Not a bad idea. The

traffic will be terrible. Won't be a better spot on Earth to see this eclipse."

At this, JR and Muzzy erupted in laughter.

FIVE

"Mary, you don't need to feel like you're Salieri and he's Mozart."

All day she had been bickering with her mother over text and every condescension and humiliation had bubbled from her memory into the front of her mind.

Mary felt like the skeleton in the Biology classroom was ogling her. She hated the creatures that crawled around her home spiting her. There was the thing that crawled around her mother—that termite that brazenly toyed with Deidra within Mary's earshot, and then there was the unseen stalker that reeked to Mary of cowardice and weakness. She feared the unseen eyes of the pathetic creature that haunted her life.

At least death did not conceal itself from her.

Her hate pulsed within her head like an ear infection. When she stuck the note on Andrei's locker she felt herself break against a wave. Her anger felt cool and she fell silent, though she knew herself well enough to understand that despite this frosty sensation she was possessed by rage. In the halls, the other students seemed to scatter around her, and her teachers ignored her in class.

"And I think this ties us into our summer reading," Mr. Miet said, "the parable 'Death in Tehran' from *Man's Search for Meaning*." Mr. Miet had a cup filled with popsicle sticks and each student's name was written on it. He would hold it during his lecture, ask questions, and randomly pick a popsicle stick out to force students to answer.

"Fallon," Mr. Miet said, calling on a girl who was president of the student body. "Can you remind us what happened in 'Death in Tehran?'" Mary thought that Fallon was a rather obnoxious over-achiever and fantasized about the student council felling her the way the Roman Senate did to Julius Caesar.

"A slave runs to his master and begs for a horse, saying that Death has threatened him," Fallon said. Her hair was tied back in braids and dyed with henna. "His master gives him the horse and the slave escapes to Tehran. Death appears to the master that evening. The master asks why Death had threatened his servant, but Death explains that he had only expressed his surprise in seeing him there when he was scheduled to see the slave in Tehran that night."

"Very good Fallon. With this in mind I'd really like to present the question, 'What is irony?'" He pulled out a stick. "Toby?"

"It's when the opposite of the way things are supposed to be happens. You know, like a fire station catching on fire or NASA actually being a priesthood."

"Do you actually think that, Toby?"

"If you want to debate me sir, I'm ready at any moment."

"Well class," Mr. Miet said, "is Toby right? About irony at least?" He pulled out a popsicle stick. He stared at it for a few seconds, then slipped it back into the cup. "I'll leave his conspiracy theory to be debunked in science class, but let's clarify something about irony. Irony is not sarcasm. Irony is closer to suspense. It is the product or effect of characters believing that they are moving towards their goal when in reality, as seen by

96

the audience, they are moving towards their undoing. When you acquire this critical piece of knowledge that the character doesn't, you become aware of the irony of the work. Irony is a texture, not a structural device like a twist. Any questions?" This whole time he had been staring at Mary, and everybody in class had caught this with curiosity.

When the lunch hour arrived she went to the baseball field hungry, stoking her anger with hunger. While she had been waiting for Andrei, her mother had been texting her, "You don't understand, you are young, you are pretty, please Mary, out in the world you're in danger.

"I am your mother, please think of me. I have to keep you safe. We don't know who did this. It could be any man. You don't know men. Please listen to me. Let me pick you up. Let me come get you. Stay with me. I'm your friend aren't I? Please Mary."

This went on all day. Mary didn't know what to write back. She tried to organize her thoughts.

As she lay shaking in bed the night before, indignation arose in her heart. She would not let herself be confined like some bird. She embraced the indignation like a pact with Baal Hammon.

She tried to articulate her feelings in a way her mother could understand. Finally, standing in front of her locker, she wrote, "After school I am going to walk to Krav Maga. Then I will come back home. I'll see you then."

Mary took her rucksack out of her locker. It was mainly composed of a worn and wrinkled black leather and her initials were sewn onto it. She slid her backpack into her locker, not on the hook as she always did,

97

but on top of the flimsy metal shelves she had installed at the start of the year. They collapsed under its weight and Mary kicked it back in as it fell out. Mary sighed and dug her cigarettes and lighter out, moving them to her rucksack with her Krav Maga clothes.

Fallon tapped on Mary's shoulder, holding a clipboard. Mary turned around and shouted, "GET OUT OF MY WAY!" The startled girl fell back, crashing into other students. Mary walked down the hall unrepentantly, indifferent to the children cowering awkwardly around her.

~ ~ ~

Photo albums once had some value. It was something to go somewhere special and take a photo. Deidra had many albums gathering dust. She had the albums that had belonged to her parents showing their town as it had been during the Korean War, during the 60s, during Nixon, Carter, and Reagan. There was something gained in taking your film to be developed in a dark room. There was something convenient in dropping off a roll from a disposable Kodak camera at a superstore kiosk.

There were albums of her as a little kid in the 80s. There was an album of photos her parents had taken of her as a teenager in the 90s. There was an album she had taken when she had dreamed of being a photographer. There was something to opening a thick white envelope filled with your imperfect, over-exposed, red-eye studded photos of your children at Chuck-E-Cheese. Then you'd store the things that mattered to you in an album under glossy plastic sheets, so that one day you'd be able to look back and remember your parents who had passed and how they held and loved your children who had grown up.

There was an album with articles she had written when she went to the University of Missouri's School of Journalism, photos of her trip to Europe after she had graduated, and one spectacular photo of her with Jonah taken in Budapest by a Japanese tourist at sunset. When that photo was taken, Jonah had just been barely more than a cute and friendly stranger. Back then she had believed herself to be in some line of expatriate succession following Gertrude Stein and Christiane Amanpour.

There were photos of a beautiful person carrying a surfboard, wearing a black vizor with pronounced cheekbones. It looked like she blinked in every photo because she shut her eyes every time she laughed. There was a photo of that young woman with Deidra in their swimsuits, seated at a table covered with a dead blue shark. Then there was a photo of those two girls dressed like Celtic maidens, braiding the long hair of a strong, dark, handsome man in a black suit of armor.

Mary came and her first two years were heavily documented with photos at her parents' house. Eventually, Deidra was waiting tables and playing piano at the mall, and she moved in with Tiffany. With help from her parents, they raised Mary, and things were never too difficult.

Then Jonah came back and Tiffany left, only to appear in the background of photos of Mary's birthday parties at home, delightful affairs where grandma would bake charming cakes.

By the time Mary and Valeria were sharing extravagant birthday parties at the Ortiz estate, there were no more photos of Deidra's friend.

In finding those albums she had uncovered the memories of Valeria and Mary that she had entirely forgotten. When she saw the photos of the two as mimes on Halloween, costumes that they ran with for five consecutive years, Deidra started to cry. She thought about destroying the albums but she held out hope that maybe one day, when time had passed and the demons had been exorcised, when the girls had grown-up, these photos might bring some little joy to them.

Somehow this made her think of the little tin boxes filled with photos that elders in Europe had shown her of provincial life. Those photos had meant the world to them. Sharing their histories had meant so much.

For all the marionettes of the world, this is all we have, Deidra thought. *So why is it that I have trouble believing that photos like these still have any place in the world?*

~   ~   ~

The Krav Maga studio was in a warehouse outfitted with a gym. Students practiced grappling on blue and red mats that interlocked like puzzle pieces. The Israeli and American flags were hung up next to each other at the front of the studio. A small group of men wearing the studio's t-shirt were seated in folding chairs.

As Mary shut the metal door, the men fell silent.

"Hey," a toned, balding man with mutton chops said. "Where have you been?"

Mary's face flushed red. "I've been busy, sir."

He shook his head. "Your mom pays too much

money for you to cut class, kid. I'm not interested in baby-sitting brats." He read her face and groaned. "Go get ready."

Mary entered the women's locker room. It reeked of anti-septic. Alex Napa, a robust woman more than a foot taller than five-foot-two Mary, was changing out of her "Winter Warlock Heating & Cooling" uniform and getting dressed. Her hair was braided tautly and hung over her shoulder.

"Testing wasn't the same without you," Alex said. They had started taking classes around the same time. Mary had never realized how much the thought of Alex earning a belt before her would sting.

"How did it go?" Mary asked.

"Fine," Alex replied. "It just wasn't the same."

That day in class they covered a number of techniques that converted the energy of attacks into joint-locks. Alex and Mary had both been quick learners and Alex had no problem quickly performing the techniques after seeing the instructor's demonstration. Whenever the instructor introduced a move with the class huddled around him though, Mary's focus would shatter like a window no matter how hard she mustered her will.

Alex would walk Mary through each move slowly, but once they tried something at a realistic pace, Mary would lose concentration again.

In the end, after they bowed out, Mary hurried to the locker room. "Mary, wait up," Alex said, following after her. "You want to go for a drive?"

"A drive? What for?"

Alex looked away, sighed, and got her things together. "Never mind."

"I'm sorry," Mary said. "Yeah, I'd love to go for a drive."

When Mary and Alex left, the sky seemed gold like sand. The guys said goodbye to them in passing and pulled quickly out of the gravel parking lot in their trucks and sports cars. The cicadas crooned. A reddish tinge seemed to float in the air and the light caught on Mary's hair. She looked up into the sky with a waxy look of melancholy.

Alex rapped on the side of her Jeep. "Mary?" She saw something in the way Mary looked out into the horizon, as if her maturity vanished into a child-like, mouth-open, happy stare. "You are a kid, after all," Alex said. Mary blushed and Alex laughed. "Hop in."

Alex had lowered the roof of the Jeep. She sped down the highway and Mary leaned into the wind.

~ ~ ~

Mary hadn't eaten at a Dairy Queen since she was little. Alex had bought them two cones of spiraling ice cream covered in a neat form-fitting layer of chocolate. From that parking lot on the hill, they could see the interstate just beneath them sandwiched between strip-malls. Past the row of ugly commercial zoning they could see stretches of the forest where the leaves of the river birches and maples breathed. She saw the river as people had always seen it when caught by the huckleberry pangs of the heart, a way dreamers had seen it since the days when mastodons lived in Missouri.

"Whatever happened to that girl who used to come and see you every testing?" Alex asked.

Mary shrugged. "We fell apart."

Alex nodded. She took a bite out of her ice cream and looked dreamily out into the distance. "Does your school ever send you on big trips, to like France or Japan?"

"Sometimes, but not everybody goes. I went to Paris one summer with some people from class."

"When I lived in Boonville, this exit was my frontier," Alex said, as if it were related. "You know, I always admired you. You were a big reason why I stuck with Krav Maga at the beginning."

"Why is that?"

"Jealousy? You're the youngest but you never back down. To be honest, I was jealous of that determined look in your eye. Somehow, watching you makes me take this stuff seriously."

Mary wanted to say something, but she didn't know what.

"Don't let the bastards beat you down, Mary," Alex said. "You're going somewhere."

Alex took Mary down country roads and side streets until it was dark. The transition had been so subtle that Alex forgot to turn on her headlights until they made it downtown. Their quiet lengthened and eventually Alex took Mary home.

"Oh hey, my dad drove a Corolla like that ten years ago," Alex said, referring to the vehicle parked on the side of Mary's house. "That your mom's?"

"No," Mary replied. "I don't know whose that is."

Alex pulled over and gave Mary a square look in the eye. They clasped each other's wrists firmly. "See you tomorrow?" Alex asked.

"Yes."

Mary hauled her leather rucksack over her shoulder and walked down the driveway. She could hear her mother playing a beautiful Celtic melody inside. Mary knocked on the door.

The door opened and Mary was greeted by somebody whose face had become worn in her memory to the point where it blended with everything home had meant as a child.

"Tiffany?!" Mary exclaimed.

They embraced each other and Tiffany kissed her on the cheek. "I've missed you so much!" Tiffany said. "Look at you. Your face looks so grown-up, but you're as big as when I left you!"

"Shut up," Mary said. "I didn't know you were coming. As they stepped inside, Deidra smiled at her, but kept playing the piano.

"I was going to come for the eclipse next week," Tiffany said, and she grabbed Mary's hand, "but when your mother told me what happened I came straight away to be with you."

"You didn't need to do that," Mary said, looking away.

"That's what family is for!" Tiffany replied. "Wouldn't you run to me if I was in trouble?"

Mary stammered, "Of course." Tiffany kissed her on the forehead.

"Tiffany made chicken adobo," Deidra said. "You must be starving."

She didn't know what adobo meant, but when they approached the kitchen, a familiar aroma brought to mind tender brown chicken, steamed rice, and soy sauce.

"Deidra, remember how the only way we could get Mary to eat was by dousing food in soy sauce?" Tiffany asked, laughing as she popped out the cork of a wine bottle. "Mary, are you drinking?"

"No, I'm—"

"Pour her a little bit," Deidra said. "She smokes, did you know that?"

"Bad!" Tiffany said. "Don't smoke, Mary."

They sat and ate happily at the table. Tiffany laughed at her own jokes and stories in a way that was almost funnier than her punchlines or delivery. Sobering footnotes followed her jokes and stories and she would quietly add on remarks like, "you know, he got Lou Gehrig's disease," or "and then she came out for Duterte and Trump."

At one point, Deidra left to use the bathroom.

Mary's fork clanked against the plate. Her eyes met Tiffany's, and she looked down at the plate.

After a pause, Tiffany asked, "Do you want to talk about it?"

Mary shook her head.

"I told your mother you could stay with me if you wanted."

Mary spun the tip of the fork around her food. "What did she say?"

"She's open to it if you are, but it may set you back a little."

Mary set down her silverware. "I'd live with you in Dallas then?"

"Well," Tiffany said, "I'll actually be in Oregon for the rest of the year."

"And school?"

Tiffany shrugged, "Your mother's figuring out something with them. You'll have to talk to her about it, but if you leave you may not come back any time soon." Tiffany grabbed Mary's hands. "You don't need to leave. This is your home." Tears welled up in Mary's eyes. Tiffany's voice hardened. "I've had stalkers," Tiffany said, unrelenting. "You don't have to give up your life to be free of them." Tiffany released Mary's hands. "Your mother's scared, any parent would be. When I talked to her today we decided that the best thing we could do is give you a choice in staying or going, and we'll help you."

"Who's ready for dessert?" Deidra asked as she came back into the kitchen.

"I am! I got this succulent apple pie in Boonville that is to DIE for..."

When they were finishing dessert, and Mary was about to excuse herself, Deidra spoke up. "By the way, we haven't discussed the lodgings."

"What do you mean?" Mary asked.

"So, when JR gets here, you'll stay with Tiffany in the guest bedroom."

Tiffany looked up uncomfortably at Deidra.

"That's not okay," Mary said.

"When Tiffany leaves after the eclipse, JR will move to the guest bedroom."

"Mom, you're not listening."

"It's simple. Your bed is too small for you and Tiffany. And we can't have JR and Tiffany share a bed."

"Can't JR sleep on the couch?" Mary asked.

"Oh no," Deidra replied. "His back needs a good mattress."

"Maybe I could find a hotel," Tiffany said, "maybe a couch surf..."

"You won't find any room available the night before the eclipse," Deidra said. "Mary, you're welcome to stay with me in my bed."

Mary imagined the bed Deidra had shared with Andrei. "Disgusting," Mary said, and she immediately followed it up with, "I can sleep on the couch."

"What do you mean by disgusting?" Deidra asked.

"Nothing," Mary said. "I meant nothing. I'm sorry."

"Uh-huh."

"I should sleep on the couch," Tiffany said. "Though you might be missing out on the rarest form of girl talk, Mary."

"Let's do our slumber party then, when JR gets here," Mary said. "I'm not feeling great. I'm going to go to my room."

"Night, Mary," Tiffany said.

"Good night."

"Good night, sweetheart," Deidra said.

"Night."

~   ~   ~

Mary changed into her white t-shirt and baggy basketball shorts, as she always did. She put on her earphones and turned the volume up uncomfortably high so that she wouldn't hear the noise from downstairs.

She did homework due for the next day and for the days that followed. Around eleven, she took out her headphones and found that Tiffany and Deidra were still raucous.

Mary finished *The Good Soldier* before the laughter died down. She lay in bed and tried to sleep. It was another night where she tossed and turned, passing hours unable to catch any rest. She lay there, listening to music, and eventually she gave up on sleep and stared at the ceiling.

Something in the way the moonbeams fell through her window caught her eye. There was something eerie and coquettish about that spot.

Mary checked her phone. It was three in the morning. She got up out of bed, slipped on her glasses, and walked to the window. She felt like she was looking into an empty exhibit at the zoo. The houses on her block had never seemed more artificial.

When she recognized this, she shivered, for an idea had planted itself into her heart.

What if I took a walk?

The skeleton flashed again before her eyes. She of course recognized how bad of an idea it was. It was foolish. It was something that she never would have done before. Mary put on her contacts. She bent close to the mirror. *Left Eye.* Her iris seemed so big. *Right eye.* She had never seen her house like this before. She wondered if she could have been dreaming. Mary felt like a small child as she tip-toed down the carpeted staircase. There was an easy trick she remembered. Supposedly, by checking time twice, a dream may be exposed. Mary decided not to use this trick. She put on her shoes. Everything seemed so big. Everything seemed to warp around, nothing more than the front door which loomed over, yet it seemed to open as if she hadn't opened it herself.

Stepping outside and shutting the door behind her, Mary felt the wind blow through her hair. The streetlamp seemed so dim and the moon so bright. Led arm in arm by her pride and curiosity, Mary took her steps down to the pavement.

The curves of the land stood out to Mary and she

followed their slithering. *To what end?* Mary asked herself. *Where am I going?* The park came to mind. If she could go as far as the park, she would come home, she resolved, though she couldn't decide whether or not running back would be a blow to her pride.

She stuck to the street, moving aside only once when she saw a car approach in the distance. Even though she moved appropriately in advance, the driver grumpily honked at her. She turned around and watched it speed violently up the hills behind her. When she had existed in that car's head-beams she had felt threatened and as she saw it leave she forgot that there was a person behind the steering wheel. There was something beast-like about the vehicle.

She was alone. Mary looked for someone, though she was unwilling to ask herself what she would do if she ran into anybody.

By the time she reached the park, however, the world had returned to a size she was familiar with. Her confidence flowed through her and she let herself rest against her pride. Mary climbed up the old cat's head slide for the first time in years and looked over the park. She laughed at herself, unable to believe that she had taken this walk and that she had made it out to be so terrifying.

Mary took a deep breath, but it caught in her throat as intuition nudged her to turn. She had strayed too far from shore. Something syrupy in her chest dripped down into a coagulating ripple. She turned her head just a bit to the side and slipped backwards, falling onto the pebbles. A man laughed at this, a man standing between Mary and home.

His sunken eyes made light of her. He was a large

man, at least one hundred pounds heavier than Mary, but maybe only five inches taller. His head and the wispy hair tied up in a pathetic bun looked like an onion. He wore a leather duster that blew out in the air. The man shook his head. He took a few slow paces forward and charged at Mary.

She screamed, frozen for only a moment, and got up, running blindly into the street away from him.

Is this who I am?

Am I a victim?

Am I prey?

Will I die right now?

Is this me crying?

Will I just be some kid everybody feels bad for?

My mom would cry. Tiffany would cry. Even Valeria would cry. Damn. Why did I have to think about that?

Valeria sometimes watched Mary at Krav Maga. "I can't believe how you subdued those dudes Mary! That was insane!"

She thought of Alex's words from earlier. She wondered if they meant anything.

I'm not any different than I was before.

Mary turned around, believing resolutely that death's face would be before her.

Her eyes were shut and wet with tears.

They opened and she screamed, not from fear but anger.

He rushed at her with his arms raised out, bent to tackle her.

He was huge.

Mary slipped. She wasn't sure if it had been on a rock or if she had just lost her footing. She dove and tackled his thigh.

Stupid.

He immediately picked her up by the waist, flipping her over. Mary tried in vain to cling to his thigh, but he pummeled her down on the ground and started punching her in the sides.

She scrambled around on the pavement and grappled his thigh. He tried to pick her up again, but Mary forced his knee to buckle and he slipped forward.

Mary had never been a promising grappler, and yet this is what her instinct brought out of her.

In those moments when the confused man tried to get himself up, Mary was able to throw her side over his chest. She landed a few awkward punches on his head, but he pushed her off of him.

Mary fell back and he bounced up onto his feet. He staggered toward Mary who thrust a fierce kick into the side of his leg that threw him off balance. Mary leapt at him from the earth like a tiger.

He tried in vain to pry her off, but even if he pulled her off a little bit, she would grab on again. He slid onto his knees, punching her as Mary tried to snag an arm.

Each punch rattled Mary. She tried desperately to catch his right arm once, twice, and on her third try trapped it. He used his weight to hold steady and dig the captive arm into her face.

Mary struggled to breathe.

She sensed his displacement of weight and thrust her knee into him, the way she had been trained for years, flipping him over in a reversal he had never felt before.

He tried to pull away, moving clumsily like a sea-lion, but Mary took his arm and fell back over him.

Her feet hovered over the ground. He tried to pull

away, quickly grabbing onto his fist, trying to prevent her from bending it back. She pulled and thrust her shoulders to the ground, as hard as she could. When his wrist slipped, her shoulders hit the pavement suddenly, before she had even realized what had happened. His scream pierced the sky as his arm broke.

She rolled away and stood up.

Don't stop, she thought, *don't stop until he's incapacitated.*

Mary took a few steps closer to the fallen man and kicked him in the head. The man screamed in pain. She pressed his face down to the ground under the sole of her foot.

The adrenaline from her fight fueled her, but the sense of danger had departed. Only her rage remained.

"I bet you're surprised," came out of her mouth. Her nose was bleeding and her lip was busted. "Aren't you?!" She dug her heel into his face. "Well, say something."

The man moaned. "Please."

"Please?" Mary repeated, and the anger flowed through her. "Is that all you have to say?" She punted his nose and screamed.

Mary stomped on his ribs. "What did you think was going to happen? Were you going to kill me? Chop me into bits? Store me in your fridge? Tie me to your radiator?"

She saw him writhe like a worm.

He was incapacitated.

He was coughing blood.

In the place pity belongs, she felt contempt. At this point it was his grubbiness that provoked her.

As soon as she realized this, she stepped away.

Mary spat on him and ran.

~ ~ ~

Tiffany decided to help herself to a glass of milk. It was four in the morning, and she had been woken by a bad dream she couldn't remember.

To her surprise, the kitchen lights were on. The open freezer door was covering Mary's head. Mary shut it and Tiffany screamed.

Mary held an ice pack against her face. She had been mashed to a pulp.

"Shhh…" Mary said. "It's alright. You don't understand. I won."

SIX

"And what was the harlot doing walking around at night when she had been warned?" the Lord Cardinal asked the mayor. That Saturday morning they walked together over Cliff Ortiz's beautiful lands. His Eminence was a tall bottle-like shape adorned in the black cassock, scarlet sash, and red hat granted by the Bishop of Rome. "Remember my son, more often than you might believe, it is they that provoke. It was wise of you to remove your daughter from her influence when you did."

The goats grazed in the summer grass as the mayor walked beside the Lord Cardinal. The Lord Cardinal was taller than the mayor and though the mayor could walk amongst even the tallest—he did coach the public school's high school basketball team—it was only in the Lord Cardinal's presence that the mayor ever seemed truly small. Even the hills and woods that the mayor enjoyed seemed like they were no longer his lands, as if the Lord Cardinal had erased property from their world.

"I am afraid, Your Eminence," the mayor said abruptly. "I'm afraid that I'm going crazy. I have nightmares every night about the world collapsing into darkness. I've seen demons dance around my daughter. I've seen horrible things that no father should ever have to endure. I fear that I may have made a mistake sending Valeria away to that therapist. There's so much pain, so much self-loathing in her eyes. She was a lion.

I couldn't learn to understand her." The mayor paused as a baby goat approached them. He pet the kid gently and lowered himself to one knee. His skin seemed so withered in the August sun. "I changed her and I fear that I have broken her. I thought I could change the city as mayor, but I can't work with city council. I feel that I've squandered my political capital trying to change this city in vain. I was wrong, arrogant, proud, and my time is coming. I should have learned to compromise and change with the world. I should have studied the example of Pope Francis—"

"Pope Francis is a fool. He bandies his words to appease heretics. He feeds Peter's flock to the wolves," the Lord Cardinal said, "and, in confidence, I shall tell you that eight hundred years ago I would have conspired with the College of Cardinals, courted the King of France, and locked him away in a cold, dark tower."

The mayor had heard of the Lord Cardinal's clashes with the Pope before, but the severity of his language amazed him.

"This isn't madness, Cliff. This isn't some psychotic mania some doctor would have you believe. No. Your dreams are a revelation." The Lord Cardinal paused and seized the mayor by the shoulder. "You can't even believe me, can you?" He smirked at the mayor. "You've let them emasculate you. They've made a woman out of you, look at me! Aren't you ashamed of your defects? You aren't crazy, Cliff. From the See in St. Louis I have borne witness to the sin of Missouri. Homosexuals! Feminism! Planned Parenthood! Political correctness gone mad is sheltering the very evils that the Church has shielded Western Civilization from for generations, and the only reason why you're seeing these visions is

116

because you're not enough of a man to stop it!"

"What can I do?" the mayor asked.

"You're the richest man in this rat-land," the Lord Cardinal said, "and the most powerful. Use that power and end this godlessness."

"Please," the mayor begged desperately, "give me guidance."

The Lord Cardinal smiled. "You are good, Cliff. You are naive and innocent, and your labors shall not go unrewarded. If you truly want my guidance, then I shall lay a path before you."

"Tell me, my Lord."

"It is no secret that without Kansas City, St. Louis, and Columbia, there would be no liberal bastion in the state. I have my machinations in place elsewhere, but you must be my knight against libertinism and god-lessness in your own domain," the Lord Cardinal said. "Bring the light of Opus Dei to the college campuses. None of this Christian youth group nonsense. I need somebody to finance the construction of Opus Dei dormitories, places where students can live with other devout members of the community, where they will be able to study in peace without the influence of maggots sheltered by society."

They approached a rock under a tree. The Lord Cardinal took a seat and the mayor rested on a knee. "My son, you must counter the illusions of crisis actors by funding pro-life PACs and lobbyists. You must drive the wedge. Sponsor radio stations, Youtube commercials, anything to hammer the evils of abortion into the minds of any voting Christian. Finally, I need your as-sistance in reigning in the Bolshevism and sodomy that has taken over the Carmelite school," the Lord Car-

117

dinal said. "You are president of the board of trustees, and your assistance will be instrumental in restoring sanctity to those once hallowed halls. What do you say, Cliff?"

With tears in his eyes the mayor looked up at him, joyously. "Yes, your Eminence, I shall do as you say."

"Then," the Lord Cardinal recited, "we shall gut the little foxes that destroy the vines."

The mayor saw the Lord Cardinal off to the Lincoln Town Car parked by the well. "Bertuccio!" His Eminence's aide had been entertained by Janine Ortiz on the patio table. He was a skinny young Sicilian with a penchant for polishing his glass-eye. His English was very good and he was so skilled in disguising gossip as small-talk that many of Janine's secrets had poured out in their conversation. The aide opened the backseat door. "I shall pray for you my son," the Lord Cardinal told Cliff before he sat down. "You are a child of God."

The Lincoln Town Car drove off, and as it approached the gates, it kicked off a storm of dust. It passed Andrei's car on the country road as he arrived.

Andrei found the estate as incredible as his first impression. *If I stuck with Valeria long enough, wouldn't this be mine?* This was an unusual thought for Andrei to have, and he laughed a bit as he noticed this.

Much to Andrei's surprise, the mayor stood by the well on the patio, smiling and waving at Andrei as he parked. With the departure of the Lord Cardinal, the mayor was able to reclaim his sense of dominance and composure. Andrei could not get the fearful memory of the mayor's tirade against him in the stables out of his mind. Though groomed and friendly, the regal personage of Mr. Ortiz threatened Andrei.

He stepped out of his car much earlier than he would have liked to, seeing the mayor approach as if to open the door himself.

"Andrei, my boy," the mayor said, "how are you?" He extended a big, hairy hand to him. Andrei had never felt a more firm handshake. "Welcome to my home." Andrei could not help but stare at his fingers. "I'm sorry," he said, and Andrei met the mayor's intense gaze. "I'm sorry for having startled you yesterday."

"Please, don't apologize," Andrei said. "I understand."

As the mayor walked Andrei toward the door, he wrapped his arm around Andrei's shoulder. "Welcome to my home. Don't ever feel like a stranger here."

The mayor led him inside. The walls were painted white and the floors were composed of beautiful hydraulic tiles that spread a simple mosaic of a flower centered on a square with stars adorning the edges.

He led Andrei into a living room that was furnished with pristine furniture. Precious Russian ceramics were stacked sparsely, yet tastefully, on a long wooden plane above the semi-circular fireplace. Valeria lay on the couch reading a book. She wore silk stockings, a porcelain white dress that covered her calves, and a yellow jacket with black adornments around the shoulders. A tight pink sash was wrapped around her waist below her chest. Her golden heels were under the table.

As Andrei and her father came in, Valeria quickly stood up. "Welcome," she said, setting her book down on the table beside white lilacs in a crystal vase. Valeria gave Andrei a loving embrace. "Did my dad find another way to scare you?" Valeria asked.

"No," Andrei said, looking up at the mayor. "Not at all."

The mayor laughed. "Can I get you anything to drink, Andrei?"

"I'm fine," Andrei said.

"Here," Valeria said, taking a few steps away, "why don't I finish giving you the tour?"

Valeria led Andrei through the corridor into the west wing. Without any lamps, it was lit only by the summer light pouring through high windows. Andrei imagined how peaceful nights must have been there.

What stood out most of all to Andrei about Valeria's room was the stained-glass window of a beautiful red-haired princess in a green dress. Its colored light fell upon the darker room with an innocence and daring that kindled a forgotten feeling in his heart. No piece of furniture in that room had been built in a factory. The pastoral wood-work of her bookshelves, her desks, cupboards, and her easel breathed the warmth and love of a creator.

It was a messy place, with books scattered around everywhere. Columns of books surrounded the feet of her bed. They were worn yellow paper-backs with dated fantasy covers and thick leather-bound editions of classics. Her desk was covered with a tarp and filled with paints and pencils scattered around sketchbooks. A canvas depicting an unfinished lamb sat on the easel.

"This is your world then," Andrei said.

"I'm sure you've figured me out by now," Valeria said. "I'm not so complicated."

Andrei walked over to the desk. He saw a large stack of papers bundled together, titled "A Door Always Open" in epic, fairy-tale font colored with brilliant pastels. The cover showed a door standing in a radiant garden. "You made this?"

"It's silly. It's called 'A Door Always Open,' except for on the cover the door is closed."

"Once upon a time," Andrei read, "a little girl chased after her dog who had run away into the woods. Her dog had smelled something unusual, something that had ceased to be in our world." He flipped the page and saw a strange mammal, something almost ant-eater like, with thick haunches and sloth-like forelegs. "It had been passing through, and had gotten its leg caught in a bear-trap. As soon as it saw the little girl, it said, 'My time is through.' But the girl was kind, so she let the creature free. As a token of thanks, he promised her that should she ever want or need to escape, a door would always come to her." Andrei turned the page, but found it blank, like the rest of the pages he flipped through.

He looked at her. She was standing in the light of the stained-glass window and he saw her silhouette. He could see her figure, her eyelashes, everything that he found desirable about her, and yet in that moment he felt like he had lost her. "Valeria, that was amazing!" Andrei said, and though he was impressed, he said it more because he had never felt so insecure of their connection. "You should finish that," he added.

"That's nice of you to say," she said, stepping closer to him. "You're the only person who's read that."

"How long have you been working on it?" Andrei asked, at ease, again confident in her affections for him.

"I started it last night."

"Valeria, that's really special."

Valeria shrugged. She took a scroll from a drawer and handed it to Andrei. As he unfurled it, he saw a fairytale play out in Valeria's stained-glass style with vignettes showing a pair of Satyr twins growing up and climbing rocks until one became enamored with a nymph. The loveless brother tried to climb a daunting mountain. He slipped near the top and tumbled to his death. The surviving brother buried his brother and left the wilderness for the plains.

"There's nothing more bountiful than a blank page. It's limitless, and for me that's paradise. It's whatever it would feel like to fly away."

"I've never had the urge to write a story," Andrei said.

"It's there if you ever feel the need to escape."

"What's it like to make it past the first page?"

"Well, it's like setting off on an adventure," she said. "You can see the possibilities and you can fantasize about the greatness of what you might stumble across down the way. After that you might get confused or hit dead ends, but that's just part of it."

"So you have trouble ending stories?"

"I have trouble finishing them," Valeria said. "I don't know, I get caught up in the feeling of possibility. At a certain point it evaporates. Everything becomes small. It's not like I can't come up with an ending. It's just that… it never feels like it's me."

"I don't understand," Andrei said, and he handed the scroll back to her.

Valeria smiled and rolled the paper up. "An ending is an ultimatum." She stored the scroll back into the cupboard and smiled at Andrei. She grabbed him by the waist and kissed him. "We should get back before my dad gets any ideas."

As they returned to the living room, they heard Janine arguing with her husband. "Cliff, you can't be serious, the kid already thinks you're nuts."

"Nonsense, he'll think it's exciting," he replied. Mr. Ortiz looked up at the stairs and smiled at Andrei. "How would you feel about eating lunch in Kansas City?"

"Kansas City?"

"Cliff, it's crazy."

"It's less than a two hour drive," the mayor said. "Andrei, are you starving?"

"No," Andrei said.

"Then what's an hour and a half going to matter?" the mayor asked. "How about it? We can spend the afternoon in Kansas City, and I promise I'll have you back here by eight."

Andrei stammered.

"I'll even let you guys have a few hours to roam around as you will!" Cliff said. "How does that sound to you?"

Valeria's eyes lit up. "What do you think?"

He thought he understood what his father had said days before about the perks of orbiting Mayor Ortiz. Andrei found himself happily sucked away into the bourgeois spirit of the Ortiz family.

"I think that sounds like fun," he said.

~   ~   ~

"... and that is how Castro ruined my family and why we left Cuba," the mayor said. He was driving them westward in his Mercedes. Janine Ortiz sat in the passenger's seat and Andrei and Valeria sat next to each other in the back. "We lived in Miami, but I couldn't stand the city. As soon as I was old enough I left home to seek my fortune elsewhere..."

123

"Cliff, can you ask Andrei a question for a change?" Janine said. "He might get the awful impression that you're a conceited person."

"Is that how I'm coming across to you?"

"Not at all," Andrei replied. "I was enthralled."

"You're too polite," the mayor said. "I'm sorry, Janine is right. I've heard that there is so much of you to note. Valeria says that you're an exceptional pianist."

"Cliff, what's he supposed to say in reply to that?" Janine asked.

"My wife is my harshest critic. Whatever criticism the newspaper might throw at me, rest assured, my wife will say something twice as critical. But tell us more. Aside from piano, what are you interested in?"

"I really like German," Andrei said.

"German?" the mayor said.

"Maybe it's not as useful as Spanish or Chinese, but I really love it."

"You say that so defensively," the mayor said. "Why should something be useful for you to love it?"

"Cliff," Janine said unhappily, taking some mysterious offense in this comment.

"I didn't mean anything," the mayor said. "Have you thought about where you want to go to college?"

"I was just going to go to Mizzou," Andrei replied. "They offered me a scholarship for—"

"Practical, economic, and close to home," the mayor replied. "Good for you."

Valeria was looking out the window. Andrei had never asked her about college. He imagined that she wanted to go to college somewhere far away, if not in the Pacific Northwest or New England, then across the Atlantic, in Scotland or Ireland.

Valeria noticed Andrei's gaze and looked at him. "Do you think you'll be happy here?"

Andrei replied with an emphatic "yes, I will," and though her question caught both him and her parents off guard, her smile let him know that she was not malicious. Despite this, the car ride slid into silence.

~ ~ ~

"Over my dead body you'll take it away!" the mayor said, and he pulled out his wallet. "I was once a busboy too, my friend." The Mayor shoved a twenty dollar bill into a young man's hand. "There! And don't report that to the waitresses, I know how they are." The mayor gluttonously dipped some French bread into the boiling buttery sauce that the escargot had come in. "Come on, try some."

Andrei reluctantly took a piece of bread and dipped it in. He was delighted by the taste. "See?" The mayor laughed heartily, almost like a pirate.

"Have you given much thought to what you want to study in college?" Janine asked.

She's like a broken record. "Well, I'm taking a scholarship for piano, but I was planning on studying German as well," Andrei replied.

"Majoring in German?" Janine asked. The servers brought everyone their French onion soup, with the exception of Valeria who drank a cold gazpacho.

"It's none of your business if he majors in German or not," Valeria said to her mother.

"That's right," the mayor said, digging his spoon into the cheesy surface of his soup. "The boy has enough time to sort everything out."

Andrei was a bit offended, but he was much more concerned with his food.

"What do you normally eat with your family?" Janine asked.

"Usually my dad and I order take-out," Andrei said. "Chinese. Thai. Mexican. Sometimes we grill hamburgers or steaks at home. My mom's a vegetarian so on weekends we're vegetarians."

"Your mom's a nurse, isn't she?" Janine asked.

"That's right," Andrei said, "she works at the university hospital."

"So how did they wind up together?"

"What do you mean?"

"If your mother is a nurse how did she wind up—" Janine shut herself up. The mayor and Valeria exchanged glances and they glared at Janine. "I mean, where did your parents meet?"

"At a bar," Andrei said.

"Oh, that's romantic," Janine said. "I mean, it's serendipitous."

The mayor interjected, "Andrei do you fish?"

~   ~   ~

Valeria and Andrei walked together down the sidewalk in the River Market. The mayor had told them to meet at Union Station at five, giving them a few hours of freedom. "My parents are awful," Valeria said. "I'm sorry. I didn't know that they'd be this awful to you."

"They're not trying to be," Andrei said.

"Are you upset?"

"Not at all."

"It's not just you. College is literally the only thing

126

my mom can talk to anybody about." Valeria paused by the window of a flower shop. "Is there anywhere you'd like to go, Andrei?"

"You lead the way," Andrei said. "I just want to take everything in."

They stepped through the doors. His stomach was completely bloated and he could not quite shake off the feeling of discomfort he felt in his conversations at the restaurant.

"You have four white roses," Valeria said, "each one unique and beautiful. Which would you pick?"

Andrei felt the flowers where the petals fondled the top of the stem. "You're supposed to feel for tightness, right?"

"One that's not fully open yet," Valeria said. "They'll live longer and bloom more fully."

"If I bought a flower for you, would you put it in your hair?"

"Of course."

"Which would you pick?"

"White daisies to match," she said, "red roses to contrast."

Valeria pulled her hand away immediately and grabbed the tip of her finger. The gash on her fingertip was jagged, curved, and deep. Blood coagulated into one thick dome.

She checked her purse and then looked at Andrei. "Do you have tissues or anything? I can't stand the sight of my own blood."

He shook his head. Valeria approached an old man behind the counter and asked him for assistance. "Oh sure," he said, chuckling to himself in an almost suspicious way, "come with me to the back."

Should I stop her? The shopkeeper is undeniably shady, but maybe it's sexist to do anything in this situation? Instead, Andrei walked around the flower shop, pausing at some orchids.

He thought of the Sarkisians and felt sad. He imagined Deidra crying again and his eyes welled up. He felt something of the pain he had caused Mary.

REPENT

If only it were that easy, Andrei thought, *that I could undo the harm that I have caused.* There was of course nothing in his power to undo the course of destitution to which he had helped send that mother and daughter. There was no restitution he was capable of or that society would ever warrant from him. *To beg God for forgiveness would be of no use to the Sarkisians at all. Whatever might befall them, am I at all responsible?*

"Oh ho ho," the old man said, emerging with Valeria, "you're a smart girl!"

"Thank you," Valeria said. Her finger was bandaged.

Well, I guess he wasn't a predator after all.

"Wait, hehe," the old man chuckled, and he toddled over to the flower Valeria had pricked her finger on. "Why not take it?" he said. He lifted it up and grinned.

Andrei and Valeria left the shop and walked to the street car stop.

"That guy was such a creep," Andrei said.

"He gave me a flower."

Is she saying that she wanted me to buy her a flower?

Sitting down at the bench, Valeria broke off the flower and tried to fasten it in her hair with bobby pins. "Are you close to anyone?"

"What do you mean?"

"For the longest time I thought you were an introvert, but the more time I spend with you, the less I find that to be the case." Andrei could tell that she was looking for a response, but he didn't know what to say, though he tried to conjure up a reply. "I feel like you can get along with anybody."

You mean, why don't I have friends? "I like being alone," Andrei said.

"Would we have ever re-connected if not for my glasses?"

"You've been gone for a while," Andrei said, "I'm sure we would have gotten along when you had settled in a bit more."

Valeria patted the flower in her hair. It was secure. "How does it look?" she asked.

"You look beautiful."

"Thank you," she said. "You know I'm not—Andrei, I know this all feels so sudden for you. I am very, very, attracted to you, but my dad really blew everything out of proportion."

"Just a bit."

"If he didn't think we were serious we'd never get to hang out though," Valeria said. "I'm sorry, my dad's crazy."

~ ~ ~

The etching depicted a man who had fallen asleep at his desk on his papers and quill. A big cat sat behind his chair, alert. A flock of loathsome owls fell upon the sleeper. There was something ever more bat-like about the birds higher up, to the point where the uppermost

129

beasts were silhouettes of demons, and there was something more feline about the owls drawn closer to the earth. It was like evil poured into the dreamer in a cascade from the unreal to the tangible.

EL SUEÑO DE LA RAZÓN PRODUCE MONSTRUOS

"When fantasy is abandoned by reason, it gives birth to impossible monsters. But when the two are joined together, fantasy gives birth to art and is the origin of wonders," Valeria said. "That's what Goya thought. I learned about it when I went to the Prado in Madrid."

They were at the Nelson-Atkins Museum of Art. Andrei had glided through the museum unsure of how to behave. He casually glanced at each painting, the way people afraid of saying "no" walk through marketplaces. Of all places he had stopped in the middle of a hallway lined with a small series of Goya's etchings, caught in the stare of two eyes.

"You went to Madrid?" Andrei asked, but he was more concerned with the etching before him.

"Last summer..." Valeria said, but she dropped this line of conversation for, "Why does it speak to you?"

"The little beast with its eyes peeking over the man's back, under the owl with its wings fanning out, its eyes are staring straight out at us."

"They're there in the middle," Valeria said, like we're supposed to look at it. Isn't that spooky?"

"I don't think I like this," Andrei said.

"Of course not. Why should you?"

"No..." Andrei found that his breathing had become difficult. He staggered back. He realized that his hand was shaking.

Valeria, who had been fine up until then, realized what Andrei was thinking about, and seeing him in such a state shook her.

"Just dreams," Valeria said. "They're just dreams, right? Why don't we get some air outside?"

"Yes," Andrei said, turning his back to the etching. "Let's go."

~ ~ ~

Andrei and Valeria sat on the great stone steps of the Nelson, in view of the lush lawn that sprawled to the street opposite Brush Creek and cascading fountain walls. They sat under the Neoclassical pillars and saw the giant weathercocks dotting the campus.

A child helped his grandfather climb down each step. They moved slowly and despite their resilience there was some uncomfortable impatience between them.

"Your problems," Valeria began, "they're not the kind of problems that you can just solve, are they?"

"They're not."

"Do you want to talk about them?"

"I can't," Andrei said.

"I suppose I can't talk about my problems either," Valeria replied. "How is it that we're only teenagers and yet we have problems that we can't share with anybody?"

"I don't know. If you had a therapist you could."

"I think that would depend on the therapist."

"What would happen if we told each other what our problems were?"

Valeria shook her head. "I don't think there's anything you could do for me. I doubt that I could solve your problem, whatever it is."

"I don't think you could," Andrei said. "I think it might sort itself out."

"Me too. If we can just make it to graduation, we're free, right?"

"That's right," Andrei said. "We're both adults, aren't we? Once we graduate, we're free, and life starts." There was a hint of cotton candy in the sky, something buried deep within. Andrei lost his grip on his previous train of thought and understood how fleeting that moment was. *Have I wasted my time?*

"I feel so bad for Mary."

"Yeah," Andrei said, realizing that he had been fighting back tears, "me too."

"It's never been fair for her. Whatever's been happening to her…" Valeria put her arm around Andrei's shoulder. "I'm at least somewhat to blame."

He covered his eyes with his sleeve. "You're not."

"Andrei?"

"It must be hard for her. Tell me," he said. "These last few days home from school, what do you think she's been doing? What has she been thinking about?"

Valeria frowned but she met Andrei's watery eyes. "I think she's been scared and lonely. That's sad, but I can't be there for her. I'm here for you though."

~   ~   ~

On the car ride back, Valeria and her mother had both fallen asleep. They rode in a long silence while the mayor sprinkled light observations about the road and the weather.

Then, out of the blue, Cliff Ortiz said, "Incentives

change."

His eyes were fixed on Andrei's. It was the strangest connection because their eyes met in the rear window. Man to man, Andrei didn't want to look away and show his fear, but in the mayor's eyes Andrei was afraid.

~   ~   ~

Night had fallen by the time Andrei walked back to his car. The mayor and Janine had returned inside, leaving the two with space to say goodbye.

"I'm sorry we whisked you away like that," Valeria said. "Maybe that's not how you'd like to spend your weekends."

"I had a great time," Andrei said.

"I was happy that we were able to spend some time together," she replied. "It matters to me." She leaned back against the well. "I want to get to know you better right now. Whatever happens while we get to know each other is a plus. Andrei," she said, practically laughing, "you can't imagine how I feel, like my old self, like I'm someone else, like I'm free. Does that even make sense?"

"Maybe I understand," Andrei said.

"What are you doing tomorrow?"

Andrei shook his head, "I have to do a project for German class with Joseph Kruger."

"Joey Kruger?" Valeria asked. She looked over at the bur oak. "Isn't he in the hospital?"

"No," Andrei said, "and he's technically still a student."

"Huh. What's the project?"

"I don't know. Joseph and I have to figure it out together. It just has to be big."

"Interesting," Valeria said, and she drifted towards Andrei and kissed him.

Andrei held her closely. "You'll tell me if something ever goes wrong?" he asked.

"Do you want that?"

"I do," Andrei said.

"I want to support you too, Andrei," Valeria said. "I'm not as weak as people think."

At last they broke their embrace. Andrei pulled out as Valeria walked inside and he cautiously drove down the dirt road, worried that he might hit some animal. He felt completely exhausted and longed for his bed. As he passed through the gates he felt an incredible relief.

"Out of sight, out of mind."

~   ~   ~

As Andrei approached his house, he noticed a black vehicle that was neither a car nor a pick-up truck. Thinking that it was a hearse, Andrei wondered what was going on at home.

He went in through the garage, so concerned for whatever might have been happening inside, that he failed to realize that his yearbooks were on his father's workbench.

His parents were in the parlor, curiously enough drinking champagne. His mother, a petite woman with wrathful blue eyes and short blond hair, was in an unusually happy mood.

"Andrei!" Ramona Goetz exclaimed. "You'll never guess what's happened. Don't worry, you're not in trouble," she said. "Why don't you sit down?"

"Okay," Andrei said, taking a spot on a loveseat.

"Your father told me everything," she said. "And I know that the issue's not piano."

"What do you mean?" Andrei asked. He turned to his father, but his father looked up at the ceiling.

"Look, I'm not a monster, okay. I get it," his mother said. "You love piano, you love Valeria, so it's awkward going to Mary Sarkisian's home. Of course. I talked to Deidra on the phone and she completely agreed with me. And she had a perfect solution." He heard a flush from the bathroom.

"Mom, I need to clarify a few things," Andrei replied.

"Honey, you don't need to come up with excuses, don't worry. Believe me, there's nothing to worry about."

"Mom, you're not listening," Andrei said. He stopped as the bathroom door opened. An impeccably groomed man with long wavy hair and a finely pointed goatee came through. His earlobes were studded with brilliant diamonds. He was dressed in a raven colored shirt with a pair of white pants and a shiny pair of suede shoes. His skin glimmered as if he had just gotten a facial treatment.

As he entered the parlor, Ramona said, "this is Ho-tah Eh-rey."

"Please," the man said, "call me JR."

"JR will be your piano teacher. Deidra thinks that you're at a level where you could grow more with him."

"I am delighted to make your acquaintance, Andrei," the man said.

Andrei was taken aback by such formal speech. It reminded him of a poorly acted play. Andrei felt like he was high and shaking hands with a Mall Santa. He felt

135

some kind of aura around JR.

Andrei's mother poured a very small glass of champagne. "Would you like a glass of Cava?"

Much to his surprise, Andrei found that she was not speaking to JR, but to himself. "I don't know about that."

"Just try it," she said.

"I'm just a little bit surprised by this cause to celebrate," Andrei said.

Henry Goetz gave a knowing glance.

"JR's the real thing," she said. "He's performed all over Europe and Asia."

JR laughed. "Minor accomplishments, I assure you."

"Stop it," Andrei's mother said. "He was a student of that Japanese lady, that famous one…"

Andrei was in no mood for bullshit and he could feel that his father harbored suspicions against this man. He took the glass his mother offered him and said, "So, what brought an illustrious piano player such as yourself to this town?"

His mother was horrified by this. Henry Goetz coughed.

JR sighed. He raised his hand out. The skin was blotchy and badly scarred. "Unfortunately, my career was cut short by a fire. I've been teaching ever since."

Well shit, Andrei thought. "I'm sorry."

"It's fine," JR said. "Don't dwell on it."

At the end of the night, when the Goetz family bid goodbye to JR, Ramona shut the door and turned off her charm. "You were horrible to that man."

"I was not horrible," Andrei said. "He's shady."

"That's deplorable," Ramona said. "This is how you treated the lady from Juilliard and that man who offered you so much from Indiana. Has it ever occurred to you that you've been offered every opportunity and you've thrown them away like a spoiled little child? And for what?" Ramona asked. "Because of that miserable girl!"

"What does this have to do with Jessi?"

"Why are you defending her?" Ramona asked. "She used you to fill some vacuum in her heart."

"Ramona," Henry interjected, "that's not alright."

"He's an adult now, isn't he?" Ramona asked. "She might have been pretty, but she wasn't normal. She was a predator, you understand?"

"What's this got to do with JR?" Andrei asked.

"The moment that wretched little girl dumped you, you gave up every ambition," Ramona said, "like suddenly nothing in the world mattered anymore to you. Is that right? I'm not going to let you grow up to be a person like that. I'm pleading with you. I've never seen you work harder in your life until you started working with Deidra Sarkisian. More than you ever did with Grushenka. You love the piano. You don't have to throw it away."

Henry exhaled. "Let's just give the guy a shot. Sure the guy seems a little fishy, but I think that's just how male classical musicians are. Deidra spoke volumes on how great he was. I trust her."

How disappointed they would be if they knew the truth, Andrei thought.

~ ~ ~

The Krugers lived in a gentrified neighborhood on the cusp of protected forest. It was a modern home unlike anything in town, designed by a famous Scandinavian architect less than ten years earlier.

There was something exhibitionist about the design, in that there were long windows that exposed much of the first floor interior, namely the kitchen, such that in spite of the trees and shrubberies that dominated the front lawn sloping down to the street, anybody would be able to see the family dine.

Andrei pulled into the drive way and parked under the branches of a willow tree. He walked up to the door and rang the doorbell, which surprised him because it made a buzzing sound.

As he waited, he could see that the inside was pristine and minimalist, though something was undeniably cozy about it. The furniture could have been from Ikea and was not gaudy, but simple and functional. In many ways it was the opposite of a story-book cottage, but it was as much of a home.

A lean man wearing the kind of spandex pants cyclists wear approached the door, smiling. He was handsome with blue eyes, a sharp jaw-line covered in stubble, and an unabashed grin. His head was shaved and he had a thick hoop in one earlobe. "Welcome Andrei!" he said after he opened the door. "I'm Joseph's father." He stuck out his hand. His accent was faintly European.

Andrei was delighted by Mr. Kruger. As he followed behind him into the home, Mrs. Kruger came down the stairs. "Hello!" she said, in an equally faint accent. Andrei greeted her and she smiled at him. "Joseph's in the backyard. I know he's excited to meet you!"

This was a bit awkward on his ears, but Andrei was increasingly open to whatever would come next.

Mr. Kruger took him out through the back. "What

did you think about your assembly this week?"

Andrei was unsure of what he was referring to for a moment and then remembered Dr. Nakayama's presentation. "Uh… it was an interesting assembly. I don't think I had ever gotten that side of the story before."

This seemed to make Mr. Kruger gloat.

A house of wood was nestled in a venerable ash tree like in a children's picture book. The tree's roots twirled into the earth and the little treehouse stood higher than the ash's lowest branches. "It's not the biggest blue ash in Boone County, believe it or not," Mr. Kruger said. "There's one in a park in Sturgeon City almost as tall as the Cristo Redentor statue in Brazil."

"Incredible," Andrei said. The sylvan sounds of the ocarina softened his heart. Joseph Kruger's legs hung from a branch over the treehouse's roof, their pale, grayish tone almost camouflaged.

"Joseph," Mr. Kruger called out, "Andrei Goetz is here."

The notes stopped suddenly and the legs and leaves shook. The boy with hair so white it seemed silver slid down gracefully. The light that bled so weakly through the leaves flitted over him. He waved and took hold of a rope, quickly sliding down the trunk. "Hey man!"

Andrei and Mr. Kruger met him by the tree.

"Welcome to my home," Joseph said. He gave Andrei a firm handshake. Andrei noticed Joseph's odd, black pearl earrings.

"Nice to meet you, Joseph."

"Call me Joey," he replied. "Thanks for meeting me here."

"Why don't you take Andrei for a walk in the woods!" Mr. Kruger suggested.

"Thanks, Dad," Joseph said. "What do you think Andrei, you up for a trip into these wicked woods?"

"Uh, I think so."

"Well, you boys have fun now," Mr. Kruger said, and he hurried back inside.

"So, Ms. Gale says that you're a musician," Joseph said, as they walked to the big black fence covered in vines at the back.

"I play piano."

"Great, I play guitar. Now, I say we make some music, something really rock n' roll."

"What?"

"For our project, for German class. We do the lyrics in German and we've got full creative freedom."

"Wow," Andrei said.

"That's what I'm saying. What are your influences?"

"Influences?"

"Yeah, what do you listen to?"

"Uh… I like… Leonard Cohen."

Joseph froze. "I like your style, Andrei. I'm feeling it already. Let's do something bluesy, what do you say?"

"Uhm… I don't think it's a bad idea."

Joseph unhitched the gate. It screeched as he dragged it across the grass. "Abandon hope all ye' who enter these gates," he said, and he raised his arm out to the dirt road that led into the woods. "After you."

"So when you say you want to make music for our project, what exactly are you talking about?"

"I think we could make an LP," Joseph said. "Or a really original music video."

"It's just… wouldn't that be hard?"

"Isn't that the point?" Joseph asked.

"Well, I guess."

"You're apprehensive."

"No," Andrei said, "I'm not… you—are you ok?"

Joseph had suddenly bent over and clutched his stomach. He walked over to a tree and took a small glass pipe from his pocket. It had been imbued with many psychedelic colors and resembled a dragon in shape. "Nausea," he said. "It's a disgrace." He put it against his lips and lit it with a small lighter.

"Are you ok?"

Joseph exhaled. "Want a hit?"

"What is that?"

"It's weed," Joseph said. "Do you smoke?"

"Not really," Andrei said—he hadn't smoked since he had last seen Jessi.

"Well, would you like a hit?"

"No, well, maybe one." Joseph handed him the pipe and Andrei took a quick hit. "Are you in very much pain?"

"Quite a bit, but I'm not any kind of Russian Fatalist."

Andrei coughed. "What's a Russian Fatalist?"

"It's when you're marching west of Moscow and you can't take it anymore so you throw yourself onto the snow and let death come and claim you," Joseph answered. "That's not me though. You like Riki Tiki Tavi?"

Andrei coughed again. He needed a glass of water. "You mean the children's story about the mongoose?"

"That's right."

"But, why?"

"Last spring I had to translate Riki Tiki Tavi into German. Why? Because I didn't know what to do," Joseph said, and he shrugged. "I was grasping at straws. I figure, if we're going to get to work together, music might as well be our best bet… I mean, what else would we do?"

Andrei nodded. "That's fair."

"I don't want to dragoon you into an Opium War with China. If there's something you'd rather do, I'll be up for it."

"Honestly I don't have any suggestions," Andrei said, "but I don't think you understand. I'm not really a musician in the way I assume you're thinking. I read sheet music and play classical music. It's not that I don't want to, it's just that I don't have the remotest idea how to jam."

"So your reservation," Joseph said, "is that you don't think you can improvise."

"I'm just letting you know."

"We wouldn't be doing anything complex or necessarily improvisational," Joseph said. "I could feed you chords and a rhythm and that's that."

"Wait," Andrei said, "so that's all we'd be doing, simple chords and a rhythm?"

"Yeah," Joseph said. "We can do the big beats digitally."

"That doesn't sound difficult actually," Andrei said enthusiastically, "in which case I have but one question. What will we call the band?"

"That's the question," Joseph said. "Should it inspire fear into the hearts of our enemies or ennoble them?"

"Why not sad and mysterious?"

"I like that," Joseph said. "We could name it after something in space, like Rigel Kent."

"That sounds too much like an English knight," Andrei said. "How about something else, and it should definitely be German."

"You mean like, Kosmonaut Träume?"

"Träume is good," Andrei said, "but maybe not Kosmonaut?"

"Mondtraum?"

Andrei took out his phone and searched for any bands with the same name. "It's no good, there's already a band with that name."

"Do you mind if I see that?" Joseph asked. Andrei handed him the phone. "Oh fuck these guys," Joseph said and he returned it, "they've got less than four thousand followers and I doubt they even believe in copyright law. Besides, it's not like we're going to be selling music anyway."

"We could though," Andrei said. The words felt as if they had slipped out.

"That's right," Joseph said, "we could, but let's not worry about slitting Hades' throat and simply focus on jacking Chyron's boat at gunpoint, at least for the time being."

~ ~ ~

Joseph sat on a wide white stump, writing in a pocket-sized notebook. "Ich habe keine Zeit zu spielen," he said as he wrote, "und zu spielen, und zu spielen. Okay so now what?"

Andrei was peeing behind a tree. "One second."

"So und zu spielen is an A chord both times," Joseph said. "Then we'll do C minor again for the next line, and then we just have to rhyme und zu spielen with something else and do the A chord thing again."

"One moment," Andrei said.

"Ich werde sterben, ich werde sterben," Joseph re-

143

plied. "I think that could be the chorus actually."

"Uh-huh."

"Want to take a break?"

"Sure."

"Do you want me to explain my sickness?"

"If you want to," Andrei said. He zipped up and walked back to the stump.

"Well I'm not dying," Joseph said. "Or at least the probability of it's pretty low. Everybody's certain I'll be better someday. The treatment's pretty much shit though. Believe me, I'd never be the type to cut school." Something occurred to Joseph and he looked curiously at Andrei. "Say, do you know Mary Sarkisian?"

"… I do."

"Did the students rally for her or anything?"

"Rally for her?"

"You know, like make a show of support."

"No," Andrei said. "Nothing like that."

"Huh. I always thought that was the kind of place St. Sebastian's was."

"Huh."

"You know, I saw her a few days ago."

"Really?"

"That's right," he said, "at the park. She was definitely cutting class. She wasn't social at all. I thought she was rude at first, but she was obviously in the midst of a crisis."

"Yeah?" Andrei said.

"You're pacing," Joseph said. He scooted over and offered Andrei some space. "What's going on with you?"

"It's not anything you could help me with," Andrei said. He sat beside Joseph and folded his arms.

"Are you having a panic attack?"

"No, I am not having a panic attack."

"It's ok, think from your wit and breathe… is this because I brought up Mary?"

"I can't."

"Oh dear."

"I fucked up."

"You fucked up? What did you fuck up?"

"Mary," Andrei said. "I ruined her life."

"Whatever it is, I'm sure that you're overreacting and being a bit too hard on yourself."

"Is that possible?"

"That's right, just say it and I'm sure I can validate you."

"I… I… I… her mom."

"Oh," Joseph said. "And she found out."

"Somehow."

"Were you at least seventeen when it happened?"

"Eighteen."

"So at least she's not a pedo."

"No, she's not."

"Was it consensual?"

"Of course it was."

"So you had consensual sex with her mother. Could that be enough to drive her into crisis?"

"I think so."

"Wait, Andrei, you don't understand," Joseph said. "My dad's on the board of St. Sebastian's and I over-heard him on the phone this morning. Mary got as-saulted when she was sneaking out at night."

"But—"

"So," he said, "she was obviously in crisis because she had a stalker or was being targeted for sex trafficking."

"I guess that's true," Andrei said, "but I still feel bad.

I mean what if I created a wedge between her and her mother?"

"You made one fatal mistake, Andrei," Joseph said lovingly and he wrapped his arm around his shoulder. "You became an adult before you became wise, and somehow you've found yourself feeling responsible for the consequences of your choices."

"I'm going crazy," Andrei replied. "I've been going crazy for months."

"Nobody knows?"

"Nobody," Andrei said, "and nobody can know. Except Mary knows and now you know."

"No worries, Andrei. I say, if it's legal, it's just provincial drama." Joseph took a hit from his bowl. "Nobody can take you to small claims court for sleeping consensually with the college widow. So what if everybody found out? People would roll their eyes, maybe your parents might start some drama, but you'll be out of the nest soon."

"I just can't deal with it."

"With what?" Joseph asked.

"The consequences."

"You made a choice," Joseph said. "Why?"

Andrei thought for a moment. "Because I wanted to make her happy. I wanted to be happy."

"So it was a valid choice, after all," Joseph said. "It stemmed from your values. It's just unfortunate that Mary was affected by it. Fuck it though. It's not your job to make everybody happy."

"So you don't think I'm a bad person?" Andrei asked.

"You really are Catholic, aren't you? Don't ask me to judge or absolve you. I don't have that power."

~ ~ ~

146

Joseph took Andrei up to the treehouse.

Simple shelves lined the walls, stacked and crammed with weathered books and worn volumes of manga. Simple wooden dolls painted with basic color schemes filled the gaps between books, all recognizable characters from comic books or television.

There were comfortable beanbag chairs, a homey desk with an electric lantern and messy stacks of paper, and a primitive little table indented with a map of Middle Earth.

"Your table's so cool!" Andrei remarked.

"We made it last summer," Joseph said. "It wasn't too tough. We projected a map onto it so we just had to trace, really."

"My dad does a lot of carpentry," Andrei said. "Now he's doing figures and stuff." He ran a finger along the spines of the books. "Did you ever get a chance to meet Valeria Ortiz?"

"We were friends in elementary school," Joseph said. "We used to read books together at the library. We played pretend together, stuff like that."

"I could have guessed," Andrei said. "You guys couldn't be more similar and yet more different. Like your houses. She lives in an old Spanish ranch in a little valley. Your house seems to be a part of the forest…"

"I remember her house. We used to pretend to be elves and we'd climb up the branches of these giant trees. One time she fell off and broke her ankle." Joseph smiled at Andrei. "Do you think she would want to hang out sometime?"

"I don't see why not," Andrei said.

"Sorry, you must be able to see that I don't get out

much," Joseph said. He blushed. "Say, do you like manga?"

"I like Dragonball, if that counts."

"Ok," Joseph said, "you're welcome to borrow my books if you want." Joseph sprung up and started tearing volumes off of shelves. "20th Century Boys. You should read that. And GANTZ. Dororo, anything by Osamu Tezuka. Ooooo... Akira! Kare Kano's the best as far as Shoujou stuff goes..." Carelessly, a little brown volume fell off. Andrei picked it up. A bizarre bird-like humanoid floated in an egg on the cover. *Berserk #12.* Joseph plucked it from Andrei's hands. "You shouldn't start there."

~　~　~

Later that evening, after Joseph's mother had brought them a little white box, Andrei and Joseph climbed to the rooftop of the treehouse. Once they were comfortably seated above the canopy of the forest, he opened it. The sun sank. "Would you like some Turkish Delights?"

"Thank you," Andrei said and he took one of the cold red sweets. "This is delicious. Could I have another Turkish Delight?"

Joseph laughed. "They're not actually Turkish Delights," he said. "It's just mochi ice cream." He opened the box and let Andrei take another. "It's just that this is exactly what I imagined that Turkish Delights would taste like when I first heard them mentioned in *The Chronicles of Narnia.*" Andrei did not understand much of this, but he adored the taste of the mochis. "Is it bad for me to call mochis Turkish Delights?" Joseph mused.

"I suppose that's a form of cultural appropriation in one way or another… I hope I'm not offending you."

"You're not," Andrei garbled, as he grabbed another one.

"Most of my friends are people I talk to on the internet," Joseph said. "They get offended so easily. I've offended so many people that I overthink things sometimes."

"You should have one," Andrei said. Joseph's hand brushed his as he grabbed one. Andrei recoiled his hand nervously. "Sorry."

"Why are you sorry?" Joseph asked.

"It's just…" Andrei said, but then suddenly, he realized that he had never seen the sun set over a forest in Missouri. He had always believed that it was something one could do in a place like Thailand or Kenya, never so close to home. Seeing the sun fall with grace into the horizon, Andrei wondered whatever could he want from an adventure, or a road trip, or anywhere far away.

SEVEN

Jason sat on his bed playing his guitar. He didn't know what to play and he didn't have the courage to play anything he liked. Jason was afraid that he had forgotten how to play anything meaningful. He wanted to stick to something safe and simple. It wasn't the complexity of the music that mattered to him—for whatever reason he could only dare to play the familiar.

> *Frère Jacques, Frère Jacques,*
> *Dormez-vous? Dormez-vous?*
> *Sonnez les matines! Sonnez les matines!*
> *Ding, dang, dong. Ding, dang, dong.*

Dave cackled from the room next door. "Why are you playing Twinkle, Twinkle, Little Star?"

Jason sighed. The odor of Berlusconi's pizza had permeated into his room.

> *Frère Jacques, Frère Jacques,*
> *Dormez-vous? Dormez-vous?*
> *Sonnez les matines! Sonnez les matines!*
> *Ding, dang, dong. Ding, dang, dong.*

Dave laughed ferociously. "Seriously, what the fuck are you doing in there?"

Jason set down his guitar. He took a few nervous breaths and shouted, "Shut the fuck up and mind your own business!"

Dave made a sound like a screeching cat. "I didn't know you were PMSing already this month," he said, and he laughed again.

Jason walked over to the door and slammed it with his fist. "Shut up!" He waited for Dave to make a comeback. Jason was certain that Dave would say something. He readied his fist to pound against the wall and tried to imagine barbarities to throw at his friend. *Why won't he say anything?* Jason thought. "Well?!"

"Well, what?" Dave asked.

Jason groaned. He sat down on his bed and rubbed his temples. He was frustrated and something was burning inside of him. He took out his phone and checked his various dating apps. He had one recent match with a college student, but he wasn't interested in her at all because of her weight. Jason quickly deleted the match and put his phone away.

The doorbell rang. "Mary," he said under his breath. He straightened his posture and hurried to the door.

Dave's sister was outside, holding her baby. He could not conceal his disappointment. "Dave, Andrea's here," he said, not even saying hi to her.

"Hi Jason," she said, sarcastically.

"Oh ignore him," Dave said from the couch. "It's that time of the month."

As she passed him, the baby reached a hand out to Jason. It made his heart jump in a way that puzzled him. Jason retreated to his room and shut the door.

He took another look at his matches on the dating app. He messaged some girls he had messaged before, girls who hadn't responded the first time. Then he picked up his guitar.

Frère Jacques, Frère Jacques,
Dormez-vous? Dormez-vous?
Sonnez les matines! Sonnez les matines!
Ding, dang, dong. Ding, dang, dong.

~ ~ ~

Mary had spent the days with her earbuds in. She had reassembled some of her father's old workout equipment in the basement and alternated between exercise and lying on the floor of her bedroom. The sweat burned the damaged flesh on her face and this only fed her anger.

She was sick of arguments with her weeping mother. She loathed the strange man who occupied her room. Having vanquished her enemy, she could not understand how she had become more isolated.

Mary had not opened her SAT book since the night of the fight. Most of her moments alone were spent basking in hatred. Unable to concentrate on school because of her own inner monologue and incapable of leaving the house for prolonged periods of time without causing her mother to break down in incessant worrying, Mary could only live in the hell of pumping iron and the following aches that rung of her own self-importance.

She lay on the clean carpet of her bedroom and stared at the smallest fiber standing up like a blade of grass. Her chest heaved. Mary turned up to face the dull white ceiling.

Where had Death gone?

By course of habit, Mary walked into her bedroom. JR was laying on her bed with his feet kicking around.

He wore wretched socks. His big toe stuck out of one sock, exposing a disgusting yellow nail.

"Oh my god," Mary said, stuck in the doorway.

JR sat up. "Everything okay?"

"Yes," Mary said.

"Did you need to get anything?" he asked.

"No," Mary said.

"I'm JR."

"Yes, I know who you are."

JR tried to smile. "I'm sorry I stole your room."

"Well, that's fine," Mary said, and she turned around to leave.

"Is it alright if I use your record player?"

"Uh…" Mary thought for a moment, "I guess that's ok."

JR hopped off the bed and opened a plastic bag on the night stand. He removed a record and quickly put it on. As he lowered the needle he said "thanks" and returned to the bed, bouncing once or twice on his butt to a piano organ cover of "Hang a Yellow Ribbon Around the Old Oak Tree" before lying back down.

Mary had entered the guest bedroom to find Tiffany brushing her hair in front of the vanity mirror. She was wearing a cute pink nightgown and had just showered. Tiffany was perfect and beautiful and Mary's face was still badly disfigured and discolored from the fight.

"Are you a vampire, Mary?" Tiffany asked. "Because I can't see your reflection in the mirror." Mary didn't know how to reply. "Don't mind me," Tiffany said. "I'm just a posh spaz."

Mary felt confused and tried to figure out what social cue Tiffany was signaling.

"What do girls listen to these days?" Tiffany asked.

"I don't know," Mary said, "Billie Eilish."

"Billie Eilish, who's that?"

"She's a girl that talks over electronic beats," Mary replied.

"That's all the rage in wedding singing these days," Tiffany said. "What do you listen to Mary?"

"Well…" Mary tried to think of what she did listen to, but found herself stammering off nothing that she really cared for and was unsure if she had actually communicated anything of substance at all, until she finally said, "I like Hole."

"I know you have a record collection," Tiffany said. "Is there really a difference between vinyl and digital?"

"Is there a difference between what you take with a digital or film camera?" Mary asked.

Tiffany laughed. *Why is she laughing?* "Well played, Mary! JR won't stop going on about your sound system," Tiffany said. "Don't worry, your mom told him not to touch anything." *Thank God.* "According to him, you really know your stuff."

"My dad did," Mary said. "That's all his stuff."

"Your dad is an expert." She turned around to face Mary and dug her hands around the chair. "So, I was thinking about going to Oregon after the eclipse for Project Pabst. I'm really close with one of the organizers there actually, so if you wanted, we could break a few laws and I could get you in and we could see Iggy Pop."

"Iggy Pop?" Mary asked. "Are you serious?"

"Yeah."

"There's no way Mom would allow it."

"She's totally on board," Tiffany said. "I wouldn't have brought it up if she wasn't. So what do you say

Mary, why don't we go for an adventure?"

Deidra called from downstairs, "Mary, one of your classmates is here!"

"Uh… one second," Mary said to Tiffany.

As Mary walked downstairs she heard a miserable voice down below.

"Has anybody told you that you look like Cher, m'lady?" Toby asked Deidra Sarkisian.

Unamused, Deidra looked up at Mary. "He's got your homework."

"That I do, fair maiden," Toby said, fishing out a manilla folder from his backpack. "Courtesy of the Nine Lords of Men."

"What?" Deidra said harshly.

"The teachers," Toby said, embarrassed by her reaction. As soon as Mary reached the door, Deidra quickly escaped into the kitchen and shut the door.

Mary took the folder and flipped through the various hand-outs. "What's this?" she asked, pulling out a thick packet of photocopied paper.

"*Leaves of Grass*," Toby said, "it's basically just a way for the intelligentsia to brainwash us with Anti-Trump propaganda."

"Uh-huh."

"And this," Toby shoved a finger into the folder. "This is important. For history, everybody was assigned a movie to analyze. Congratulations, you got *Godzilla*."

"What do I have to do?" Mary asked, flipping through the paper.

"It's straightforward. You need to say what *Godzilla* means in its historical context. What it was trying to say. It's about revisionism. Or visionism. Whatever. You got the easiest one."

"And what did you get?"

"*Three Hundred*," Toby replied, "directed by Zack Snyder."

"Well, thank you," Mary said, shutting the folder.

"I was thinking—"

Mary rubbed her forehead. "It's too early to invite anybody to the prom, Toby."

"I'm sorry," Toby said in a way that provoked Mary.

"Why are you sorry?"

"Whatever you had to go through… If you ever need anything…"

"Thank you for bringing this folder to me," Mary said.

Toby shook his head. "I hope you'll come to the eclipse on Monday, Mary." Toby bowed his head a little bit and stepped out.

As Mary shut the door, she looked into the kitchen and saw her mother talking on the phone while she read some tarot cards on the table. "I'm seeing a Fire sign enter your orbit. Aries, Leo, Sagittarius. Now…"

~ ~ ~

Mary's second visitor came unexpectedly. Mary was on the rowing machine, listening to the same song on loop that she had been listening to all day.

"Mary, somebody's here to visit you," her mother said. "One of your friends."

Do I have friends? Mary thought to herself. She walked upstairs, half-expecting to see Toby again.

It was Alex Napa from Krav Maga.

Perhaps struck by Alex's impressive stature or their stalwart forearm handshake, Deidra did not object when Alex asked Mary to take a walk.

The air seemed to vibrate in the heat. Mary deliberately walked the path she had taken on that night, finding that the space had shrunk considerably and that the neighborhood reminded her of a movie set.

"I'm proud of you," Alex said. She kicked a Styrofoam cup paces ahead of her on the curb. "Everybody's proud of you from the gym. The old man says he wants to know when you'll come back."

"Did he really?" Mary was blushing. "The truth is, I don't know. I might be leaving town for the next couple months, to clear my head a little."

Spots of sunlight fell on the tree bark and leaves. The lawns were cast in large swaths of shadow.

"Where would you go?" Alex asked.

"On a trip with my aunt. She's not really my aunt but she might as well be," Mary replied. "She wants to drive to Oregon."

"I don't blame you. When you're ready we'll be here for you." Before Mary could thank her, Alex changed her tone. "Are you ok?"

"Am I ok? I won. I'm more than ok"

"In your head, I mean," Alex said. "Before what happened, happened?"

Mary sighed. "Definitely not."

"Do you want to talk about it?"

Mary shook her head. Perhaps it was her pride or shame, but Mary felt summer sluggishness strip her will to speak. "I wish it were that easy, but it's not."

Up ahead a little sparrow had been picked apart by crows. Alex noticed that Mary's gaze was caught on the miserable affair and she yanked her by the arm. "When you stare at somebody for too long they're going to assume you're interested and check you out. Where are you taking us anyway?" They had been retracing each of Mary's footsteps from that night and Mary didn't understand her own motives.

"The park," Mary said.

Alex frowned. Her worried expression slowly quivered until she laughed. "You are the type to sleep on the bones of your enemies!"

Hearing Alex's laughter, Mary found herself joining in. At least for a moment, her moodiness and sulking seemed humorous. Though she was not embarrassed at all, she felt a remarkable acceptance for her vindictiveness.

When they reached the park they found a sad little boy fiddling with a bicycle.

The little boy looked pitiful. "The chain's stuck."

Mary approached the boy and squatted down. She fiddled with the chain, but it was too taut to move. The more she struggled with it, the more her hands became covered in a black grease. She fiddled with it for minutes without a word.

Finally, with one big tug, she made the chain move fluidly.

"Thank you," the little boy said. He took out a piece of bubblegum wrapped in paper. "You can have this."

Mary shook her head.

"No, seriously," the little boy said.

Mary's hands were entirely black and so, to not taint his hands, she extended an open palm. The little boy dropped it in her hand and said goodbye. As he rode off, Mary raised it up to Alex.

"Mind opening this for me?" Mary asked. "My hands are nasty."

"Yes they are." Alex unwrapped it. "Open up," Alex said, and she set the block of gum on Mary's tongue.

As they left the park Alex asked Mary if she thought any good karma would come out of it. Mary said that she doubted it, but Alex could tell that there was happiness in Mary's voice.

"When was the last time that it felt like the world didn't owe me an apology?" Mary asked. She chewed on the gum slowly and felt each light step kiss the earth. "Alex," she said, and now there were tears in her eyes and her voice became rough, "why can't the world feel like this every day? I've felt this way before and I've always lost it. I will always lose this feeling, this feeling which is like being loved by both your parents as a child, before sex, before politics, before the magic goes away."

Alex Napa pulled Mary clumsily into an embrace. "I wish it was easier," she said, "but it's the way things are. You'll always get jealous. You'll always feel left out in the right circumstances. You'll always hear somebody's thoughtless words and feel them follow you to the grocery store. I'm sorry that it's even harder with the big things. I don't know how a world can be as violent as ours and yet the only thing that can make us feel truly safe is when we let ourselves love it. I don't know Mary," she said and she pulled away. Alex looked into Mary's brown eyes and cried. "I wish that it was easier. We just have to live for those moments when we feel safe in the world."

They returned to the Sarkisian house while Deidra was giving a piano lesson to a kid from down the lane. Alex and Mary sat at the edge of the bathtub while Mary scrubbed her hands under the faucet to remove the grease. Alex had worked up a concoction of sugar and water that was making steady work of the filth.

Tiffany popped her head into the bathroom. "Hi girls!" Her hair was filled with little white flowers.

"Hi Tiffany," Mary said awkwardly.

"Who's your friend?" Tiffany said, smiling at Alex.

"Uh, this is Alex from my Krav Maga gym."

Alex smiled. "Alex Napa. I do HVAC and refrigeration repairs."

"A handy-woman," Tiffany said. "How nice. Speaking of which, what happened to your hands, Mary?"

"Uh…"

"Mary fixed a kid's bike."

"Good for you Mary!" Tiffany said. "Do you mind if I sneak around you and pick up the aloe? JR took me out on his new kayak and I got a little burnt."

Moments after Tiffany was out of sight, Alex whispered. "Who's that babe?"

"Uh…" Mary said. "That's Tiffany, she's my sort-of-aunt that I told you about."

"She's sexy."

"Stop," Mary said, with a hint of viciousness in her tone.

"I'm just kidding!"

~   ~   ~

Jason had spent the day messaging every woman that he had ever hooked up with or dated in town. Some were married, others had moved, and the rest ignored him.

He couldn't get those fantasies out of his head. He imagined her a little older, putting red lipstick on in a clean, decent bathroom in a St. Louis condo. He imag-

161

ined her in a short black dress mounting him with alcohol on her breath saying, "I need you. I need you."

He had downloaded every major dating app and had given up after spending a half-hour on a more dubious platform.

Jason could see the foam from her splash as she dove into a swimming pool in Los Angeles. He imagined Mary sprouting through the surface to shake her black hair. He could see the red swimsuit barely covering her curves.

Surely I can find a nice Romanian prostitute in Mid-Missouri, he thought, but he quickly shrugged it off. *Better jerk off before making any decisions I regret.*

He had a frozen pizza in the oven which had hardly thawed before he had thrown it in. Jason checked on the timer. *More than enough time.* Though he tried he couldn't get Mary's bottom lip out of his head. The urge to bite it consumed him. It was fat and juicy and he could see every line on it pop out crisply.

He went to his bedroom and picked up his V.R. headset. Jason sat down on his bed and scrolled through videos on a porn site. He stumbled on a young actress with black bangs, a small athletic frame, and narrow curves. He slipped the phone into his headset, then realized that he needed lotion.

As he walked to the bathroom, he could hear the door open. He froze in the hallway and saw Mary come in.

"Jesus Christ!" he said, seeing the beating her face had taken. "What happened to you?"

"I got into a fight," Mary said.

"I can see that." Jason stroked his beard.

Mary offered him a wrapped gift.

"I don't understand," Jason said, taking it. "Why? Mary, what's—"

"Please open it."

They walked to the couch as he tore off the paper, carelessly tossing it to the cluttered floor. Jason stared at the box, failing to understand what it was, until he was seated firmly. "You got me a guitar pedal," he said. "Why?"

"You'll need it, won't you?" It was one of the models her father had shipped to her.

Why would I need it? Jason almost asked, but he couldn't release the words. Never before had Mary seemed so beautiful to him and yet half her face was repulsive and marred. In that half he could only see her vulnerability to the world. For all that vulnerability, Jason truly understood that he was not Mary's equal. He was an older man who benefited from the fact that she wanted cigarettes and saw something redeemable in him, something redeemable if only for a lack of redeemable qualities. It hit him then that he was just a dewdrop clinging to a blade of grass and soon he would vanish without a trace from her.

"Hey Mary, what's going on?" Dave walked into the room, quickly restoring Jason's composure. Dave was wearing a yellow jacket, the kind of vest made of cheap fabric that glowed in the dark. He froze like a gazelle and said, "Jesus, Mary, and Joseph, what the fuck happened to your face?"

"I got in a fight."

"Well fuck, you look like a ghoul."

Mary wiggled her fingers like a kindergartner playing a ghost.

"Are you working construction again?" Jason asked,

abruptly changing the subject. He was twisting the tip of his beard into a point. *Jason's doing a lot of beard-stroking,* Mary thought.

Dave shook his head. "Nah, it's new policy at Berlusconi's. Everybody's got to wear one, even if they're just driving."

"That barely makes sense."

Dave shrugged. "It's the funniest thing. Everybody at work claims it was their idea. Somehow it's caught on as a great idea and nobody seems to agree on why we have it or what the point even is."

"Oh hey, Dave," Jason interjected, desperately wanting to forget what had just transpired in his heart. "Guess who Mary saw the other day." He casually set the pedal down by his foot.

"Who?"

"Annabelle."

Dave cackled hard.

"You said she got put into a mental institution."

"Yeah I mean, that's what the family said, but a few months ago, when I was at Nash Vegas I ran into her brother's ex-girlfriend and she said, wait for it, that she was possessed."

"Possessed?" Jason said and he started laughing.

"No it's true!" Dave said. "At first they'd just catch her arguing with herself and then one day she quit her job and started stalking some rich kid. Kid." He pointed at Mary. "Your age. Eventually he got so creeped out by her that a restraining order was issued. She was sectioned after that and when they let her out she was basically bonkers and surviving off of SSDI." Something about this made Dave chortle. "Well, kiddo and kidette, I've gotta get to work."

Dave left the two in silence and finally Jason realized that whatever had transpired in his heart had rippled out. Mary had undeniably changed in the last few days; he felt as if her perception of him shifted.

"Hang on," Jason said. "I left the oven on." Jason left Mary alone and walked to the kitchen. He checked his cell phone and looked anxious as he typed. He sent his message and turned off the oven.

"Do you want to know how I had my first panic attack?" Jason asked. Mary had never seen him so nervous. "I had a fish bowl and I realized that the water at the bottom couldn't circulate. You can't put big fish in a fishbowl or they'll suffer. It's hell for them," Jason shook his head. "Some people stick to the bottom and no matter what they dream or how hard they try, they get caught here. Then there's the people who get trapped here because they care. The worst are the people who leave, because their shit always makes it back here... But I suppose I'm saying that out of jealousy. Will you remember what I said when you're in Harvard and somebody shits on Missouri?"

A gust of wind pushed open the door to the back patio and a McDonalds bag blew across the floor like a tumbleweed. The floor was so filthy and it occurred to Mary that Jason's bed and sheets were always so clean, clean like his fish tank. He was capable of cleanliness and accountability, and yet she had made him out to be some wounded bird.

The house, the man, and his choice of friends had suddenly lost the tinge of being adult, edgy, and different. It was nauseating and suddenly she felt the need to go. In a moment she lost the will to take care of him. It pained her to realize that the whole time she had viewed him as a hill not worth dying on and that her care for him had been indulgent and self-destructive. Understanding this, and recognizing his humanity, Mary felt an urgent need to cut ties with him altogether.

Frère Jacques, Frère Jacques,
Dormez-vous? Dormez-vous?
Sonnez les matines! Sonnez les matines!
Ding, dang, dong. Ding, dang, dong.

Perhaps, like with cigarettes, she knew all along what she had been doing to herself. Pity colored her vision and she could no longer remember what this place had meant to her. She was disgusted by the idea of being who she had been before the fight. Mary longed for Tiffany's world, the impossibly ideal and free vision of Iggy Pop at Project Pabst in Portland.

It was then that the doorbell rang.

"I'll get it," Mary said. She had every intention of leaving without saying goodbye.

"It's ok," Jason said and he walked to the door.

Spikes of anxiety drove into her nerve endings. "I need to get going anyway," Mary said.

"Huh?" Jason replied, following her to the door.

A beanstalk State Trooper stood at the entrance. He was younger than Jason, but so tall that he could bend his spindly body over to have his face at Jason's level. The State Trooper wore a pair of aviator sunglasses over a vampire bat-like nose, which together with his diamond jaw and cocksure smile formed the composite of masculine beauty that had grown inextricable since 1980 from Plato's ideal of the jackass. Most ridiculous of all was his trooper hat, which framed his asininity.

"Afternoon," he said, "I'm Officer Aaron Fuhrman. I'd like to come in and ask you a few questions."

"What's a state trooper need with me?" Jason asked.

"I need to ask you a few questions," the State Trooper replied. "Can I come inside?" Noticing Jason's hesitation, the State Trooper smiled handsomely and said, "No worries, anything I'd find in there would be Fruit of Poison Tree and I wouldn't be able to charge you for none of that."

"Well," Jason said, "I have no reason to doubt a First Responder at his word."

The State Trooper nodded politely, slinking by Jason. "Hi Little Lady," he said to Mary. "That your girlfriend?" he asked Jason.

"N-no."

"Young," he said, practically bending over the top of her head, "but seems legal. Can't blame you." He looked over into Jason's room and noticed the Confederate flag. "And you've got Ol' Dixie hanging up."

"Southern heritage," Jason replied nervously.

The State Trooper waved his hand. "I like you Jason. You mind if I call you Jason?"

"No—of course not, Officer."

"Jason, it's not too common these days that you meet a man that gets it. Tell me, would you mind fetching me some water?"

"No, not at all," Jason hurried off ridiculously to the kitchen. As soon as he was out of sight the State Trooper grabbed Mary's cheeks and turned her face, muttering something indiscernible as he stared at her. Mary stared at him helplessly in horror.

He took off his glasses, revealing two innocent, squinty eyes. "It's ok," he whispered, "I'm handsome."

He let go and patted her on the cheek. "Just play along now and it'll be alright."

Jason returned with a bottle of water. "It wasn't in the refrigerator, I hope that's—"

"Fine, fine," the State Trooper said, as if it were a major inconvenience.

"So what's the trouble, Officer?" Jason asked.

"What's the trouble?" the State Trooper asked, pretending that this question had been stupid. "I think she knows. I mean, not to take the Good Lord's name in vain, but, Jesus, have you seen her face?"

Jason became pallid. "What?"

"Relax Jason," the State Trooper said, "we just need to figure this out. I reckon we all should take a drive."

"Why? I don't understand why you need me."

"Shush, shush," the State Trooper said. "I don't want to get a warrant. I don't want to press no charges. Jason, I'm from hills and burroughs and I'm used to settling things like a man. Common sense. Love. That's what this country's all about. Hell I'm more on your side than anybody else, so believe me when I'm saying that we can do this the easy way or the hard way."

"Alright," Jason said. "Where do you want to go?"

"We'll just take a ride."

"I really should get back home," Mary said, "is the thing."

The Officer laughed and shook his head. "She thinks I'm an idiot. She's gonna come with us too. I'm trying to keep her mother out of this," the State Trooper said to Jason. "You can understand, can't you? Don't worry, she'll be fine."

"I think we should do what he says, Mary."

The State Trooper grinned.

He invited Jason to sit in the passenger's seat, leaving the backseat for Mary. As they drove, Jason appealed to the State Trooper, to the point where he mentioned that he had voted for Donald Trump.

"Did… did you serve by chance?" Jason asked.

"I did," the State Trooper replied. "Straight out of high school."

"Thank you for your service," Jason said.

"Never forget," the State Trooper replied.

As it got dark they were south of town in an unrecognizable area.

"Where are we going?" Jason asked.

"To a place we can talk," the State Trooper replied.

He pulled over at an exit by a state park. "Come along now," he said, stepping out. "Tell the girl to stay in the car for a second."

"Hang on, Mary," Jason said confidently. "I'm sure it'll just be a second."

The State Trooper walked around to where Jason stood. "Would you turn around for me?"

"Um?"

"Turn around for me."

Jason did as he asked.

"Put your arms behind your back."

The State Trooper handcuffed him. "I want you to sit down there. Mary Sarkisian," his voice boomed, "step out."

Mary nervously stepped out. "I don't understand."

"Turn around!" he shouted.

Never before had she felt so weak and violated as when the State Trooper trapped her in handcuffs. The tension between her wrists as a consequence of the chain was overwhelming. That moment of submission humiliated her. It was like being confined by her mother, only she could not dare to challenge the authority that subjugated her.

"Officer," Mary said, "can you explain why—"

"Can I explain why? This isn't story time," he said, which shut her up.

Mary Sarkisian believed that she was an insignificant bug before the will of this State Trooper. The State Trooper ordered them to walk down a trail in front of them and followed behind with a flashlight.

Most shamefully of all, Mary began to believe that she had actually done something unforgivable, that Jason had done something equally unforgivable, and that they were deserving of whatever the State Trooper had in store for them. Mary believed that the State Trooper was worthy of being Judge, Jury, and Executioner, and in this respect, resistance was not just futile but somehow wrong.

The State Trooper sent them off the path and up a hill where two men waited for them with shovels. They had finished digging a hole, a few feet wide, a thoughtfully dug hole.

One of the men was short and stocky, built like a wrestler. He wore a Punisher shirt and a pair of blue jeans. The other man was barely an adult. He was tall and lanky with a mohawk.

Mary realized that they were staring at her, not with lust or animosity, but a strange curiosity.

The State Trooper and the men looked nervously at each other for a long moment, until finally the State Trooper yanked Jason and pushed him down on his knees, facing Mary.

"I want you to know," he said, "that whatever happens here tonight is firstly between us, second that's it's all because of you, and third, and this is the important thing, it's for your own good."

Mary stammered. "What's for my own good?"

"You don't understand," the mohawk kid said, genuinely trying to appeal to her. "Nobody's leaving until you accept the light of Jesus into your heart."

Mary stammered.

"Hush," the State Trooper said. The man in the Punisher shirt handed him a bible. "We need you to find Jesus at the very least."

"I don't understand—"

The State Trooper kicked Jason in the face, leaving him quickly bloodied.

"Every time you speak out of turn," the State Trooper said, "I will hurt this man. Now where were we? There was a man who was much like us. I never knew him, but I am certain he was no different than any of us. What they found in his home proved it! He was onto it. He had been given the same dream."

"I don't know what you're talking about!"

"There it is!" The State Trooper said. He took out one of his keys and grabbed Jason by the hair. He viciously tried to wedge the key into the hole of his ear gauges. Jason screamed in pain as the State Trooper wound up his arm to thrust it in multiple times.

"PLEASE STOP! DON'T HURT HIM!"

The State Trooper shook the bloody key at her. "You don't understand! This is your fault! Every time you open your mouth he gets hurt. I'm trying to help you. They are trying to help you. All you're doing is hurting him."

Mary was crying now and avoiding Jason's stare.

"I know you're not trying to hurt him or anybody else, but this isn't Catholic School. Intention won't save you or any of us. Neither will so-called works. You are putting us all in peril. Why? Because you lack faith. Jewishness won't save you. Catholicism won't save you. The Church won't save you. Only faith matters. I think if you have genuine faith by the end of the night, everything will be ok. What matters is that we save you. So let me ask you, Mary Sarkisian, do you accept Jesus Christ as your Lord and Savior?"

"YES!"

"LIAR!" the State Trooper yelled, and this time he tore so hard into Jason's ear that he severed the lobe.

Mary shrieked.

The State Trooper kicked Jason down on the ground. He pulled out his gun and aimed it at the back of his head. "I will kill him if you scream again. That blood will be on you. So now tell me. Do you believe in God?"

"Yes!"

"You're just saying that to save your own skin. Seeing this man suffer… That doesn't inspire anything in you? Can you not feel compassion? Love?"

"Of course I do," Mary wept.

"How?"

"I would do anything," Mary sobbed, "to make his pain stop. He doesn't deserve to be hurt like this. It's not right."

The State Trooper put away his gun. He shook his head and spat on the ground. "No, you don't get it. If you don't know Jesus then you don't know what love is. You are putting wants ahead of needs. It is momentary pain versus eternal joy. It is damnation versus salvation.

The so-called hurt you feel? That's just your selfishness. You don't want to be confronted with somebody else's pain. It makes you feel guilty, but you're a coward, Mary Sarkisian. You would rather have a coddled life-time and a hellish after-life. Salvation requires making the tough decisions in this life, girl."

Mary stared down at the dirt in front of her. She knew it wasn't a dream. There was no escape from that moment. As she stood there in her hand-cuffs she wanted nothing more than to be in her own bed.

Mary wanted to be home, a child again in the arms of her mother.

"You think we're stupid, don't you?" the State Trooper said. "Well let me tell you something. Your schooling won't teach you nothing that matters. But they'll fill your head with nonsense and none of it will actually make you better than me. There are only two truths: God and America, and being American means loving God. So whatever bullshit you thought, this is America. You'll never be better than us. We're the ones in charge. Who's in charge?"

"You're in charge."

"Who does America belong to?"

"You."

"I believed that," the State Trooper said, happily. "I'm doing something for you Mary. I'm teaching you how to think with common sense. That's nothing your school will teach you how to think with. How you see the world right now. Everything's so vivid and clear. It's like being a child again. No nonsense theories to cloud it. That's how life is supposed to be. That's how you find God. It's so easy to because God's Truth is real. Your doubt is on the wrong side. Do you get it now? Jason, what do you think?"

Jason had also been crying. He was shaking considerably and suffering from a panic attack. "Mary, I'm so—"

The State Trooper quickly whisked his gun out and barked at Mary, "Come along now!" The State Trooper grabbed Mary by the hair and lifted her up. "COME WITH ME!" He pulled her by the arm and threw her against a tree stump. He aimed his gun at her head. "Not that it will save your sorry life. But do you now, before your death, accept Jesus as your savior?!"

Mary let out an even deeper sob. "I don't want to die!"

"That's not what I asked."

"I'm so scared," Mary cried. "I'm so scared."

The State Trooper looked into Mary's eyes. "Do you accept Jesus?"

Mary stood in darkness and grasped.

"YES!"

He put the gun away. "I believe you."

"What?"

"Guys, I think we did it."

"What did you do?" Mary asked before erupting in sobs again. She fell onto her knees, never having felt so worthless in her life. The State Trooper pulled her up and dragged her back across the hill.

The kid with the mohawk was bandaging Jason's ear. The stout man himself was rubbing his eyes with his arm and turned around. "He'll be fine!" the State Trooper barked, but his voice betrayed his own sadness.

Mary fell. The mohawk kid walked over to Mary and tried to pull her up. Mary was limp. He struggled with her for a second.

"I'm sorry… I'm sorry," Jason said.

~ ~ ~

On the car ride back, all Jason did was cry and say, "I'm sorry. I'm sorry."

The State Trooper pulled over into a fast food parking lot. He walked inside, leaving Mary with the two men.

When the State Trooper returned with the food, he passed a bag out for each one. Mary sat with the greasy bag on her lap, staring blankly at her knees.

The kid with the mohawk passed an envelope to Jason. "Here's what you were promised."

Promised what?

"We gave you a few hundred extra."

The hatred and anger that had characterized her last few days returned to her, this time cold.

How much?

When to her surprise she realized that they were driving back to her neighborhood it became evident that they truly believed that they succeeded at something.

They pulled over a few blocks from her house.

"Don't bother calling the cops," the State Trooper said. "Nobody will believe—."

"Jason," Mary said, ignoring the State Trooper, "how much did they pay you?"

"Go ahead Jason," the State Trooper said, "how much?"

175

Jason looked out the window. "Eight hundred dollars."

Mary stepped out and walked home.

I'm worth eight hundred dollars. The light of the setting sun seemed to extinguish itself as she reached her home. Her mother and her friends were laughing in the kitchen and Mary quickly rushed back to the guest bedroom and threw herself under the sheets.

> *Frère Jacques, Frère Jacques,*
> *Dormez-vous? Dormez-vous?*
> *Sonnez les matines! Sonnez les matines!*
> *Ding, dang, dong. Ding, dang, dong.*

The sound of laughter wafted from the halls of her home and though Mary wished she could cry in her familiar bed, she could only soak her tears in impersonal sheets. "Tie a Yellow Ribbon Around the Old Oak Tree" was playing from her bedroom and all she could do was weep as a stranger. *I'm worth eight hundred dollars.*

EIGHT

Andrei parked outside of a piano shop that rented basement rooms to musicians. The piano shop was in a small retail center, a small coterie of restaurants and a high-end grocery store, just a short drive from St. Sebastian's. JR stood against an El Camino stretching his back in a swimsuit and a tank-top. He was eying a woman dressed in yoga clothes who was loading a sack of groceries into the back of her Jeep. "Need a little help, miss?"

Andrei sighed and waited for the song playing on the speakers to finish before stepping out of the car.

"Good afternoon, Andrei!"

"Hi."

"I was thinking," he said, "why not spend today getting to know each other a little bit? I talked to your mother and she thought it was a good idea."

"I don't understand."

JR rapped in the inside of the El Camino's bed. "Look inside." He pointed at a kayak.

"You want to go kayaking?" Andrei asked.

"Don't worry, I'm not charging a nickel. Seriously, I'm no snake-oil salesman, Andrei. I want to earn your trust."

"I guess that's fine."

"You ever been kayaking before?" JR asked. Andrei shook his head. "You'll pick it up. Come on, get inside."

As Andrei got into the car he thought how much nicer life would be if he was the rebellious type. The front seat was littered with audio cassettes and CDs. JR brushed them onto the floor. When he turned the keys, the sounds of "Take Me Out to the Ballgame" on a baseball organ started to play over the speakers.

"Is this what you normally listen to?" Andrei asked as JR pulled out.

"Always. I used to listen to... everything. I know this kind of music might seem trite, but once I stopped fighting it, I realized that it was much happier—I was much happier. You know what makes people unhappy, Andrei?"

"What?"

"Noise," JR said. "The sounds in your head that go, 'I should have done this,' or 'I should have done that.' We love to make ourselves suffer with idle chatter, but with this kind of music you don't have to think, you just let it move through you."

Andrei was thoroughly uncomfortable with all this and did not see how this could go well for him. His mother was fine with JR, and apparently Deidra was fine with him, but Andrei felt unsafe.

I should at least try to understand this guy. Andrei looked around for a conversation piece. He didn't want to talk about the music anymore, but he didn't know what else to bring up.

"How did you burn your hand?"

JR lowered the volume and sighed. "It wasn't an accident, not some freak accident. There was a fire and I chose a person over my hand. Not even my hand. Just some flexibility. Not a bad deal as far as sacrifice goes." He looked at Andrei and pointed to a round tin in a cupholder. "You mind opening that for me?"

It was chewing tobacco. Andrei unscrewed the lid

and JR plucked a piece out. As he chewed, he cast Andrei a few looks. "So, what do you want to ask me?"

"Do you normally talk like that?"

"Like what?"

"I'm sorry."

"Is it my tone? My cadence? It's my word choice, isn't it?" JR asked. "I can't help it." He smiled and shook his head. "I tried my hand at acting. Never had a career in it, but I wanted it. Took lessons. Took it all seriously. Did Renaissance Fairs. Between those I did sales. Experience made me talk the way I do. Yes, Andrei." He lowered the window and spat out. "I talk like this."

He waited for Andrei to say something, then after a minute, raised the volume up again.

Andrei spoke just as JR turned the knob. "How well do you know Deidra?"

JR lowered the sound. "We used to move around a lot. We travelled around together, the three of us, Tiffany, Deidra, and me. Do you know Tiffany?"

"No."

"We lived in a beach community for a while. Deidra went home. Got pregnant. Didn't see her for years. Tiffany helped her out for a while before coming back to live with me."

"Was she your girlfriend?"

"Yes and no. Not really. We had our differences and went in different directions."

"So you're a drifter."

"I," JR said, "used to be. Then I found God. Now I drift purposefully."

"So you found faith?"

"No. Not faith," JR said. "Faith is beautiful, but I don't have any of that, outside of what I place in the

179

future. As far as gods and monsters go, I only believe in what I have seen and heard."

~ ~ ~

The kayak moved swiftly down the Missouri River. Andrei found it easy to maneuver. It was just a matter of moving in rhythm with JR. The sounds of the river and the birds brought peace to Andrei's mind.

Maybe I've misjudged JR, Andrei thought.

For what it was worth, Andrei was having a good time.

Summer shimmered over the land and the light reflected from the water as if off of a dragon's scales.

They pulled over by a small cave on the shore to eat lunch.

Andrei dried his hair with a small red towel, stopping for a moment to take a bite out of a peanut butter and jelly sandwich.

JR removed a melon from his backpack and sliced it open with a large knife. He cut it into several thick slices. "When you want it," he said, before taking a slice for himself. "It's the little things in this world that deserve the most love, don't you think?"

Andrei agreed and took another bite from his sandwich. JR had packed an inordinate amount of peanut butter and jelly under thin slices of white bread. They ate their sandwiches in silence, looking at the river.

His slice of melon was so wet and sweet that he had another. *Don't I belong to life? What if my worries were for nothing? Everything has turned out fine for me and this world has done nothing but show its resilience and love for me.*

"Sometime soon," JR said, in a quiet, breathy tone, "on the day of the eclipse, your life will change." He spoke at the cave wall and Andrei didn't immediately catch what he was talking about. "There will be an unforgettable moment," JR went on, turning to Andrei, "that may seem like an eternity, but when it is over, whatever happened in that moment will have vanished like mist, completely untraceable, I promise you. You will move on from that and your life will be free from the troubles that have bothered you." JR took a bite of his sandwich. "Go on, eat."

Is this happening?

Andrei stammered and tried to explain to JR that he did not understand. JR interrupted Andrei with his hand and looked curiously up in the air, smiling. "I can hear them—echoes." JR squatted in front of Andrei and ran an index finger horizontally in front of Andrei's face.

Andrei wanted to leave that cave. He eyed the kayak and asked himself how far this would have to go for him to be justified in running off.

"So you've had dreams," JR said. "Valeria, she's had them too. You've figured that out by now, but neither of you have had the courage to bring the pieces together. I know your secret, Andrei, and I promise you that it will be buried. All you must do is what the universe asks of you."

Andrei looked at JR with a frightened bewilderment.

"… What…?" Memories of night terrors came to Andrei's mind.

"To betray your conscience for the sake of our world," JR said. He lowered his finger. "Tell me, what is

181

Christianity to you?"

Andrei swallowed. He nervously shared the story of the lion and the Christian he had told Valeria earlier that week. Every few lines JR would make incredulous or mocking faces.

"That's what Christianity is to me," Andrei said, ashamed, "it's about mercy and love."

JR shook his head. "Look, you've missed the point. That's not even a story in the Bible. Tell me, are you familiar with the story of the Binding of Isaac?"

"... Yeah."

"Abraham took his unknowing son up the mountain and quite outside the boundaries of reason moved his knife to slay his son. It wasn't that Abraham was a pawn in the game of a petty or sadistic extra-terrestrial. It was that he was able to build a bridge between himself and God. This bridge is what we call faith. It isn't belief. The truth of this world is that once you find this faith you are free and every action you take is done as a free man. Do you understand me?"

Andrei chewed on his food silently. He felt scared and a little filthy. *Should I run away?* Every instinct within him suggested that JR was delusional and even dangerous, but some sliver of thought lured him in. The truth was that everything could make sense if filtered through JR's prism.

"But I still haven't explained what is wanted of you," JR said. "I'll show you when we're back to the truck."

JR was silent on the kayak-ride back. Andrei felt befouled. The trees and wilderness seemed to be part of a hostile and haunted world. Something in the sound of his paddle strokes reminded him of conquistadors on the Amazon.

When they reached the shore, JR and Andrei walked through cattails and approached the El Camino. Andrei's skin had been singed by the sun and his arms ached.

JR pulled a guitar case from behind his seat. He set it down on the ground. "Go on, open it."

Andrei unfastened the hinges and opened it.

There was a sword in a blue sheathe inside. Its hilt was thin, striped in white and blue, with even grooves running along it, and a metal rod for a cross-guard. There was something innocent to it, as if it could never be used for any evil. The simple thing sang of heroism.

"It's yours," JR said, "or it will be on the day of the eclipse. Go ahead, take it out."

Andrei lifted the sheathe up, surprised by its lightness. He drew the sword out of it, satisfied by the sound it made as it became free. Andrei moved it up into the sun and saw the light dance off of its steel. JR took a few steps back.

"Go ahead."

Andrei looked at his feet and back to the sword. He swung the sword up and down awkwardly, struck by the ridiculousness of the situation. He wanted to leave.

"Here," JR said, and he took a step closer toward Andrei, "try swinging it like this." Andrei imitated JR's movements uncomfortably, and with each moment he felt more desperate to leave. Andrei swung awkwardly, cursing his lack of self-esteem.

~   ~   ~

Half-way through their drive back, JR pulled over. "I might have pushed myself a bit too far by carrying the kayak," he said. "My back is in a lot of pain, quite suddenly. Can you drive and drop me off at Deidra's house? It couldn't be any more than a ten minute walk from the piano shop."

Andrei drove uncomfortably. He could barely focus on the road as he thought of his promise to Mary Sarkisian in the dugout. JR prattled on about the Muppets and Andrei felt like he was getting a migraine.

Andrei parked on the street. His palms were sweaty.

"Can you help me inside?" JR asked. "I might need some help. I'm sorry."

"I shouldn't go inside."

"Why not?"

"Mary. Mary can't stand me. It wouldn't be right."

"Mary wouldn't be here now. She has Krav Maga. Nobody's home."

Andrei sighed.

"Ok."

Andrei helped JR up the stairs. He was shocked to enter Mary's room. It was nothing that he expected. The LEGO pyramid and record collection all seemed like something that would belong to a friend of his.

As soon as JR was on the bed Andrei tried to excuse himself.

"Do you mind putting on a record?" JR asked, stretching himself out on the bed. Andrei was intrigued by Mary's collection and quickly delved into her records, surprised by the precise similarities of their taste in music. "No, no," JR said. "It's not there! The case on the speakers."

Andrei did as JR asked and picked up a record titled, "Take Me Out to the Ball Game! And Other Hits."

"Thanks, boy," JR said after Andrei set down the

needle. "Tie a Yellow Ribbon Around the Old Oak Tree," played as Andrei stepped out into the hallway, eager to get away as soon as possible.

Mary was standing there slack-jawed. Andrei was appalled by the damage dealt to half her face, seeing something scaly or reptilian in it.

"I'm leaving," Andrei stammered. "JR needed help."

"YOU—" Mary charged at him and shoved him against the wall.

"Stop!" JR shouted.

Andrei raised his hands up submissively.

"Mary, it's alright!" JR said, raising an arm out to her from her bed. She looked at him in disgust. "He's with me. I asked him to help me."

"What a disgrace," she said, lowering her fist, her hand still on Andrei. Feeling his chest heave as he nervously took a deep breath, Mary dug her eyes scornfully into his.

"Get out!" Mary shouted.

Andrei quickly ran down the stairs. He fumbled with the lock as he opened the door. *Should I say sorry?* He leapt out onto the porch, the door swinging open behind it.

~ ~ ~

Andrei parked behind a new Subaru stacked with bicycles on the back. From the sidewalk, Andrei could hear the Gipsy Kings playing from inside the Krugger house.

Mr. Krugger answered the door holding a glass of white wine. "Andrei?" He was dressed in a free-breathing white shirt and a pair of slacks.

"Hi Mr. Krugger," Andrei said. "Joseph said I could come over, is that—"

"Of course," Mr. Krugger said, "some friends of ours from Cologne are staying with us."

The guests were lounging in the living room, bantering happily in German. Casablanca was playing muted on the TV. Andrei was surprised to see a keyboard mounted and Joseph messing around with an amp, a guitar strapped around his shoulder. Joseph waved him over. "This is Andrei," Mr. Krugger announced to his guests in English, "he is a student of German and is working on a musical project with Joey."

"Guten Abend, ich bin Andrei."

The Germans clapped.

"Very good," Mr. Krugger said. "This is Gaby, and this is her partner Nadja."

"How do you do!" Gaby said.

"Wow," Nadja said, "how do you do!"

"And this is Joey's godfather." One of the tallest and most muscular men Andrei had even seen stood up and offered him a handshake. He looked like a Soviet boxer. "G.F."

"G.F.?"

"Golden Fingers," Mr. Krugger said, and the Germans erupted in laughter.

Joseph interrupted gleefully. "What do you say we debut our new sound to the world?"

"What do you mean?"

Joseph set some papers on the keyboard.

"I transcribed it for you," Joseph said, and he tilted his head to the side.

Andrei, unsure of how he felt about the whole thing, sat down.

The sheet music had been transcribed digitally. True to his word, Joseph had made use of practically only four chords, with some deviations. The lyrics accompanied the notes, which Andrei knew meant that Joseph had gone on without him.

"We ready to go?" Joseph asked.

"Uh…"

"We are Phillip Traum! One, two, three, four!" Joseph went ahead with the opening chords.

Phillip Traum? I thought we agreed on… Andrei followed suit, finding the expectations of his fingers to be quite low, if not boring, yet he found something uniquely exciting about the direction the movement went as Joseph started singing and the music came together.

There were only four chords, but he was having so much fun!

Holy shit, Andrei thought, *this might be the greatest thing I have ever participated in in my life.* He looked at the guests. *Fucking shit they're dancing! Golden Fingers is… they're all having a good time! People are listening to me play music and they're having a good time!*

Andrei looked over at Joseph beaming. Joseph raised his eyebrows and mouthed "sing."

Andrei nodded and they busted out the chorus in unison.

The song ended with the same lyric and the vibe was so strong that they repeated it continuously along with the audience.

When they finally stopped, the Germans erupted in cheers. Golden Fingers was out of breath from dancing so hard.

After exchanging some pleasantries, Joseph excused them from the gathering.

They went downstairs to the basement. It was filled with vintage arcade machines. A trendy bar stacked with various liquors was lit by a greenish light. Familiar 19th century advertisements for absinthe and tobacco decorated the walls.

As Andrei told Joseph what had transpired that day, Joseph played a *Star Trek: The Next Generation* pinball machine.

"What he said about Abraham and Isaac doesn't make sense," Joseph said. He pulled the knob and the plunger fired a ball off. "That story's used to illustrate the leap of faith. Unless… could contemporary Christianity have bred consequentialism and utilitarianism into… of course… Nicene Christianity places faith in the resurrection and not in wisdom."

"What are you saying?" Andrei asked.

"I do really well at pinball when I speak and focus on speaking. I don't even know what I'm really saying." The ball eluded the flippers and sank. "See?"

Andrei looked at the score. "Well it seems like it works."

Joseph pulled the knob again. "It is the resurrection that validates the wisdom, not truth that validates itself as the Gnostic Christians believed before they were murdered by the Nicene Christians." The ball ricocheted across bumpers and flew up a ramp. "So faith for them isn't actually faith, it's trust. Trust in a narrative, no different than the trust you and I place in history. Therefore consequentialism and utilitarianism are bred like a horse to a donkey and the result is instrumentality. DAMN IT!"

He missed the ball and it slid through. Joseph

turned around to face Andrei. "You should cut off all contact with these people," Joseph said. "This JR guy is obviously suspicious."

"But it checks out," Andrei said. "I've found videos of his performances on YouTube."

"Regardless, there's only trouble there. Is there anything you're not telling me?"

Andrei stammered for a moment, then confessed the bit about the sword.

"Why would he offer you a sword?"

"I don't know," Andrei said. "I mean, he didn't actually give it to me."

"Why did you hide that?" Joseph murmured. "Never mind, he obviously has ulterior motives and none of them could be good. What if he tries to fuck you?" Joseph grimaced and then more quietly said, "Or tries to get you to suck him off?"

"Ok," Andrei said, ignoring Joseph's last question, "look. I have been having dreams lately."

"Uh-huh," Joseph said.

"Really bad dreams. Where demons quote the Bible at me."

"Uh-huh," Joseph repeated.

"I think the same thing is going on with Valeria Ortiz and JR seemed to confirm this."

"How did he know?"

"I don't know. I didn't say anything when he told me all of this."

"So you think he's right," Joseph said. "You think that something is going to happen tomorrow and you will need that sword."

"Right."

"So he'll go to school and give you a sword? We

should call the cops."

"Well we wouldn't be going to school, we'd be at Mizzou for the eclipse."

"We could still call the cops."

"You don't even need a license to own a gun in Missouri. Why would they care?"

"I don't know. You could tell them that he tried to suck you off."

"I'm not going to tell the police that he tried to suck me off!"

"Ok, ok, fine. I think that there's an easy solution," Joseph said, trying to calm Andrei down. Joseph picked up a backpack and slung it over his shoulder. "We'll figure out a way to handle this ourselves. Let's go outside."

~ ~ ~

As soon as they passed through the gate an owl hooted. Cool swatches of purple and blue parted the night sky. The blue flowers in the woods stood against the dark. As they tread the path Andrei felt like had recovered some sense of innocence or perhaps he was simply remembering what companionship was. Though his life had never seemed more uncertain, the grace in the stars stirred a feeling within his heart, something so separate from the instrumentality of cell phones and standardized testing. He had only known it in fantasy. For however troubled he was, he could only feel curiosity and wonder.

"Why do you think people have sex?"

"Because they're lonely and neglected."

"Do you actually think that?"

"Well, Jessi liked me, because she was alone in the

190

world and nobody really knew how to listen to her, and Deidra, Deidra realistically speaking, probably something similar, and then it's probably safe to say that with Valeria…"

"If what you say is true, then does the person even matter? Couldn't they have all just fucked the milkman?"

"If the milkman knew how to listen," Andrei replied.

"So you know how to listen," Joseph said. "Is that your superpower? You know how to listen to women and that makes them want to have sex with you?"

"Are you saying that they were disingenuous?"

"No… they were probably… ingenuous, but they definitely were using you to fill some gaping emotional hole."

"Why me?" Andrei asked.

Joseph took a puff from the pipe and then shook it three times at Andrei. "I believe," Joseph replied, "that you are dependent on a sense of validation that makes you not push these women away. You are sensitive, quiet, and a good listener. People in pain trust you, and naturally feel like you will understand them and give them some reprieve from suffering. You don't want to fail anybody. So when somebody's humanity becomes wrapped up in yours, you need their validation as much as they might need yours."

"Damn," Andrei said.

Joseph took him up a steep slope to the top of a bluff overlooking the forests and the river. "I'm not a psychologist though," Joseph said. "I'm also really high." Joseph took another hit and passed the bowl to Andrei. "Here's one thing I do understand, Andrei. This thing called romance is a way to rationalize brain chemicals.

It's no different than astrology rationalizing life through movements of stars. It's why we have extremists. There's no substance to it no matter how far you develop the concepts. Chemistry's no way to find happiness in life. All it's good for is managing pain and having fun. What I think matters, at least, is what makes you truly happy, and I think that takes substance."

"I'm not sure I agree, Joseph," Andrei said, "People need religion. They need ways to rationalize everything or they'd go crazy."

"Maybe you're right," Joseph said. "Who am I to give advice anyway?" He plopped down and dangled his legs off of the cliff. "You can see the Milky Way out there, can't you?" Andrei stood next to his friend and gazed into space. "In Japan, it was customary to see the Milky Way as a river. There were once two inseparable lovers who were split apart. They live apart from each other divided by the river, except for on one day, when the same fate that separates them lets them stand together. There!" Joseph shouted. "Can you see that?"

"Of course."

"No, can you see that?" Joseph asked.

"See what?"

Joseph thought to himself and unfastened one of the black pearl earrings.

"Try this on."

"Why?"

"Just try it." Joseph held it out in front of Andrei.

Andrei removed his stud and dropped it into his shirt pocked.

He took the pearl and, as he touched it, a strange feeling flowed through him, as if he were put under at the dentist's.

"Put it on," Joseph said, but the words sounded glossy and went past Andrei.

Andrei groggily looked at Joseph and smiled.

"Here," Joseph said, and he took it and fastened it to Andrei's ear.

"Fuck!" Andrei said.

His clarity came back to him, only everything he saw and felt seemed so crisp. He caught the thickness of the air entering his lungs and felt a sudden wind shift.

"Can you see it now?"

Oddly enough he saw a mist move through the trees, several mists, and with each moment they seemed to him familiar in the form of elephants.

"Mastodons?"

"Let's go to the stream," Joseph said. "Shall we?"

Speechless, Andrei followed Joseph down the rocks along the brook.

As they reached the bank of the river, Andrei saw an ethereal mastodon raise its trunk from the water to spray its back. He froze, seeing the texture of its hair become visible out of what had been a cloud-like thing. Joseph clasped his hand and suddenly, like a switch had been flipped, night became day. The trees scattered themselves, shifting. The river veered, contracted, and expanded frantically. The mastodon became firm and living. Amber inked its coat.

They heard the voices of people speaking up ahead in the old indigenous language.

Joseph let go of Andrei's hand. Dark returned and the mastodon became again ghostly.

"Come," he said, and he took out a small, heavily beaten bowl made of silver from his backpack. He knelt by the river and captured some water. "Sit down beside me. Look into this cup."

"Why?" Andrei asked as he sat down

"Answers," Joseph said. "If I can make it work." He stared at it for a minute then exhaled and shook his head. "Let me try again in a few minutes." He set down the cup and loaded his pipe.

"Can you explain?"

"Years ago my parents put me in an extra-curricular reading program," Joseph said and he huffed on his pipe. "I had a tutor who was then a teenager called Annabelle. Annabelle was kind and pretty and I always liked her. That was that. I never saw her again. That is, until this summer when I found her by chance in the woods. I had just found my ocarina and I would go after day-break far off the beaten path to create something that truly belonged here.

"Whenever you bring a pipe of weed into the forest there is always the chance of meeting Stoner Fairies, so it was no surprise to me when I noticed a girl sitting on branches."

Andrei interrupted. "What's a Stoner Fairy?"

Joseph shook his head. "It's nothing magical. It's what you call a girl you meet on a hike that's down to smoke weed."

"I'm sorry, please continue."

"She was a free-spirited and wild girl. She had long brown hair crowned with holly. She wore a green dress that made her look like a dryad. She was sitting up on an oak tree."

Andrei gasped. "Did you fuck this girl?"

"Patience my friend," Joseph said. "She was watching me play the ocarina and I was as enthralled by her as I was by the opportunity. When I finished playing my song, she clapped, I bowed, and then I offered her some hits from my pipe." He passed the pipe to Andrei. "When she fell to the Earth and drew closer to me I immediately recognized Annabelle. As she spoke to me I was so certain of it. After we smoked for a while, she looked up at me from the pipe and batted her eyes. She lunged at me and we tumbled into the dirt. That is how I lost my virginity."

Andrei clapped. "A triumph for the Senate and People of Rome!"

Joseph sighed. "Had it ended there," he said, "surely it would have been. I was so certain that whole time that it was her. Obviously it was a surprise when, as we lay naked on the Earth, smoking and talking idly, she suddenly got up and got dressed. I asked her if I had met her before and she shook her head. I asked her what her name was and she said 'Erubira.'"

"Erubira?"

"Yeah, so I asked her if she had changed her name. She laughed and said, 'bye Joey,' and then she ran off into the woods."

"Did you see her again?"

Joseph shook his head. "The whole thing was weird, but sex completely changed my priorities in life. I wanted to see if I could run into her again, so I went on walks in these woods for weeks. Eventually I gave up. Then in July, on a ridiculously hot day, I was alone in this janky park by the hood and I got this really uneasy feeling. I turned around and I saw Annabelle standing there, staring at me. I quickly met up with her, but she had changed, she was much more sullen and she had lost a lot of weight. She was still pretty, but it was obvious that she had gone through a rough patch. There was nothing of the nymph in her.

"I said, 'Hey Annabelle, what's up?' and she shook her head and said, 'My name is Erubira, this is my dummy.' As we spoke her weight and beauty started to return, so subtly I didn't notice until minutes had passed and I was suddenly attracted to her again. We did it again, but once I had finished I was immediately overcome with disgust in myself. She spoke of the weirdest things, not understanding space or time very well. The more we talked the more I was certain that there was something off with her and that I might have slipped into a very bad situation. She was, I suspected, mentally ill, but I didn't want to believe it. You see, she was very beautiful and despite the red flags I struggled to let go. It was thus a relief when she left without a warning.

"These kind of encounters went on this summer and I slowly got some coherent idea of how she identified. She believed herself to be a visitor from somewhere far away and that Annabelle was something she occupied. In other words Annabelle was either possessed or thought herself to be possessed. I believed that she was delusional until one afternoon after we had sex she realized that I was lost in thought. I actually was hating myself and realizing that I was in denial about the whole situation, but instead I lied and said that I was concerned about my future on account of my illness.

"She became very concerned and asked me to come with her into the woods to a stream. Oddly enough, this very silver bowl was lying there against the rocks in the water. She knew exactly where it was. Erubira filled it and asked me to look inside."

Joseph swallowed, "I saw my death, my death and

burial. I didn't like that, not at all. I was devastated and burst out crying. She embraced me and told me to calm down, that it would be alright. She promised that she would prevent it. Then when I was calm she ran off again, leaving me with the bowl.

"It was a very painful week later. I tried to use the bowl to see into the future but it was no use. When I was in the backyard, I saw her standing, gaunt and tall, by the gate to the forest. I felt very apprehensive about letting her in, even though my parents were away, because this had become my great secret in life. When I approached the gate, though, she had become so young, my age. Undeniably a girl, and never had I seen her so beautiful before. I let her in. As we kissed in my garden everything seemed to flourish, it was incredible, it was magic."

Joseph tapped on his earring. "Then she gave me these, promising that these would give me health, that they would keep me safe from death and make any of my dreams come true. When she had gone, I tried my luck on the silver basin again and this time I was able to make things appear on the other side. I mainly saw cosmic phenomenon and I wasn't able to manifest anything purposefully. Then, by chance, I made a connection.

"The being on the other side didn't appear to me in any form. I could feel a loud vibration go through me and I would see what looked like a vibrant blue star on the other side," Joseph blinked as he said this and wrinkled his nose. "It was very friendly and we communicated back and forth the way people kind of do over ham radios. It was very basic communication, but we were confused half the time because our basic assumptions were very different. Eventually I tried to explain to him what had happened, which took an entire night—like we'd get hung up on the most basic things like the fact that humans need to rest and what a house is. Anyway, once he understood what was going on he warned me that Annabelle was in fact occupied by a thing called Erubira and it was very, very important to banish her.

"He offered me a method, which to my surprise was a shared concept: The Extraterrestrial Banishment Ritual. It was essentially a dance. My body shook as if I had been shocked and I just knew how to perform it."

Andrei shook his head incredulously.

"What do you mean a dance?"

Joseph stood up and demonstrated. He put his hands on his waist and pushed his butt out a little bit. He took a few steps around as if he was square dancing. He waved his hands to his left and to his right and clapped. Joseph raised a knee and hopped around. Then he stomped his foot down and pushed out his hands.

Andrei started laughing hysterically. He had not laughed so hard all year.

Suddenly Andrei felt as if he was about to vomit. He thought he was keeping it back down, but in a moment he realized that he was choking.

"What's wrong?"

Andrei coughed out a mess of black tar onto the ground. He tried to take a breath, but he vomited out more of it. After a third expulsion he could breathe.

The black tar coagulated. It unnaturally gravitated together into the form of a hideous baby that crawled upward into the air as if it were going up invisible stairs. It stared into Andrei's eyes.

The black tar erupted into each direction and faded away.

"Jesus Christ!" Andrei said, spitting as much as he could. He lowered his face to the river.

Joseph, who was quite terrified himself and shivering, quickly hurried to Andrei's side. "No don't do that," Joseph said. "That's not good water."

"What do you want me to do?!" Andrei tried to ask but his tongue seemed to trip over itself as he was reminded of the nastiness that had just left his body. He babbled for a minute and then fell onto his side as he was crying. Joseph embraced him the best he could and their earrings vibrated furiously, wrapping each other in a sphere of white light.

"MAKE IT STOP!" Andrei shouted, and Joseph quickly let go.

"I'm sorry," Joseph said. Then Joseph noticed that the water in the silver bowl was glittering. "Hey! I know now's not the time, but the bowl's working."

"This is horrible," Andrei said.

"We can stop," Joseph said. "We probably should stop."

"No," Andrei replied. "Just get it over with."

"Okay," Joseph said.

Andrei curled up in the fetal position facing the bowl.

The bowl caught the reflection of the stars. They waited a long while, and right as Andrei tried to speak Joseph shushed him. Finally, as Andrei's mind had drifted off, something, an acorn or a pebble, seemed to fall in the basin. The water seemed to turn to liquid metal.

"That was lucky," Joseph said, and he quickly began

to stir the water with his hands. "I don't fully under-stand this, Andrei, and I don't know what we will see." Joseph grinned and peered into it. "What should we ask him?"

"Maybe we could start by asking him what the fuck is going on!"

Joseph shook his head. "No, we have to be more literal than that or he won't understand us."

"Please," Andrei said meekly.

Joseph nodded. "Ok. How about… 'Are Andrei and I in danger?'"

"What did he say?"

Joseph looked dumbly at the bowl. "He asked who Andrei is."

Andrei rubbed his forehead. "Who the fuck am I anyway?"

"Relax, this star's a genius, when you get the right words in," Joseph said. He concentrated firmly on the water. "Ok, I think he understands now. Yes, we're in danger."

"That's great."

"When are we in danger?" Joseph asked, as if it were a Magic Eight Ball. "Tomorrow. Andrei's in danger. Not me."

"What?" Andrei crunched deeper into his knees.

Joseph shrugged. "It's the eclipse. You can't escape it."

"Why not?"

"I don't know, something to do with killing the calf."

"That doesn't make sense, Joseph," Andrei replied. "Your friend isn't helping by speaking in riddles."

"Relax Andrei, maybe he can hear you."

"Joseph, I don't want to die. This is terrible."

"Can we avoid all this?" Joseph asked. "Yes, we can."

"How?"

Joseph smiled. "He says it's very simple. All we have to do is hold hands while each of us wears one of the earrings and you won't get sucked away into wherever it is that you'd have to kill the calf."

"That's it?" Andrei asked.

"Yup," Joseph said, "and everything would be ok."

"Great," Andrei replied. "So we'll hold hands. When are we supposed to do that?"

"When the eclipse starts."

"Precisely when though?"

"He doesn't understand seconds or minutes, Andrei."

"Ok, so fine, we'll just hold hands all afternoon?"

Joseph bobbed his head back and forth. "Yeah."

The bowl lit up.

"Ok, so he's telling me that the calf-killer could choose to ignore that advice and kill the calf because there are valid advantages to doing it." Joseph was flummoxed. "Something about reducing plastic? And what if he refuses to kill the calf? Then everything will fall apart."

"So what's the point of holding hands?"

"The point," Joseph explained, "is that you wouldn't get whisked away to a scary sub-dimension for a few minutes. That's where the danger is!"

"I don't understand."

"Ok, so, basically, you can either kill the calf and the world will be as it always has been, only somebody will cross over," Joseph said, "or you can not kill the calf and everything will change and the world will be unrecognizable."

"Why?"

"I don't know," Joseph said. "But don't do it Andrei. If you kill somebody tomorrow, you're a murderer."

"The calf's a person?!"

Joseph wagged his head. "Uh, likely it is."

"Can you ask why this is happening?"

"Ummm…" Joseph thought for an unusually long moment. "It's not Erubira who's tampering with reality. It's not her ritual. It belongs to that of a craftier extra-terrestrial."

"So it's unrelated to you and Erubira?"

Joseph wrinkled his nose and blinked. "So Erubira might one day try to find me again, but whoever is doing this has no idea that I exist."

"So it's unrelated?" Andrei said.

"I don't know," Joseph said. "Here's the real question. This seems to corroborate JR's claims. If that's the case we need to find out what exactly JR is—" Joseph sighed. "I'm sorry."

"About what?"

"The connection went out."

Andrei turned away to his other side. "Can't you call him back?"

"No," Joseph said. "I don't think so."

"What was that stuff that was in me?" Andrei asked.

Joseph shook his head. "It was extraterrestrial, but nothing like Erubira."

"Dummy," Andrei said, "do you think it was trying to make me into a Dummy?"

Joseph swallowed nervously. "I think that we can't know right now, but it was certainly lower level than Erubira."

"What are we going to do tomorrow?"

"What were you going to do tomorrow?"

Tears fell from Andrei's cheeks to the dirt. "The field trip."

"So," Joseph said, "why don't we drive together? We'll live a normal day and hold hands through the risky bit and then we'll go on with our normal lives."

He set a hand on Andrei's shoulder. "Does that sound like a plan?"

"Yes," Andrei said, "that sounds like a plan."

With that last syllable, Andrei broke down. He was cold, the world felt cold, and Joseph's hand was the only warmth he could feel.

NINE

Valeria Ortiz was born with strings attached to her back. She was beautiful, blond, blue-eyed, rich, and born to the most powerful man in town. She was the descendent of Cuban and Slavic emigres and no matter which way you traced her lineage, you would find class and nobility.

On the day of the eclipse, these strings which would have lifted her one day to a suite at the Estadio Metropolitano where, as a representative for the Wanda Group, she would nonchalantly bribe the Mayor of Madrid into privatizing public housing, were cut. She would be wearing a black dress, a long, white, cashmere coat, and the only person more beautiful would be her reflection.

Early on the day of the eclipse, Valeria shut her locker. Fallon stopped behind her and scornfully addressed her. "Hey, I wanted to say that I read what you sent Mary and I think you're trash."

Valeria blinked.

"Actually," Fallon continued, "you really represent everything wrong with America."

Valeria's blue eyes wavered as she tried to look blankly back at her. She waited patiently for Fallon to leave. Everybody in the hallway stared at them.

She met all the faces with defeat only to find that they would look away as soon as their eyes met.

Valeria would see much of the world she had already seen, only through different eyes, sometimes with migraines or with a slight stupor. She would learn several languages and become good at them. Her biggest surprise would be finding that she had remarkable customer service skills. Eventually she would learn how to solve any problem diplomatically.

Valeria Ortiz would become a flight attendant for Emirates. A few nights into her training she would fully reclaim the sense of freedom and devil-may-care attitude she had lost after the incident. At first she would not become close to any of her cohort, but she would smile at them with such relentless expressionism that they would worship her as an idol of radiance and humor.

Her eyes would light up as they hadn't in years. Valeria would never be sad once she slipped on her heels, put on her Emirates red hat, and tucked the scarf into it exactly the way determined by procedure.

Nobody in the history or future of the airline would be as good at folding the scarf as Valeria Ortiz.

Valeria took her seat on the bus surrounded by the baleful eyes of her peers. She took a deep breath and straightened her posture.

This is the world I live in.

Valeria dug her nails into the plastic seats as she passed the vindictive stares. This world felt as alien as the texture of the cushions.

The worst they will do is talk.

She remembered the blowing of a fan on a hot summer day. Her feet rested at the end of the frame. Valeria stared up at the ceiling for an endless while. "Stop," Valeria said, and she pushed away the hand.

What's wrong with friendship?

Politics made such clean boundaries of everything

to everybody. Once a boundary between two people is blurred, restoring it is like separating ink from water. *What can you do but burn a bridge?*

"I love you."

"Take that back."

How could the touch of a moment's exploration change everything? It could even move backward in time and defile the past.

Valeria shuddered and looked anxiously at the front of the bus, dreading Mary's possible appearance. Andrei had messaged her earlier saying that he would go independently with Joseph Krugger.

Joey...

She recalled the face of a little boy and their adventures in the woods. She remembered the worlds their imaginations had created.

Toby boarded the bus. Through her blurry vision she could see the fuzzy red mass on his head that she knew could bear no words other than MAKE AMERICA GREAT AGAIN. Toby smiled once he noticed the empty seat next to Valeria. *Please don't sit next to me. Please don't sit next to me. Please don't sit next to me.* As soon as he touched the back of the seat Valeria shook her head. "Don't sit next to me, Toby." The students were all watching this and it bothered Valeria to think of how the her in their minds was becoming naturally bonded to the concept of Toby.

Toby frowned. "Sorry," he said, wounded. "There's nowhere else to sit."

Valeria looked out the window and scooted toward the edge of the bus.

Toby took his seat.

"I'm sorry V, I won't say anything. I can take a hint."

"Take off your hat," Valeria said.

"What? Why?"

"If you're going to sit next to me, take off that hat."

Toby was flabbergasted. "Are you embarrassed—"

"You're going on a field trip, what do you need that hat for?" Valeria replied. Her face had flushed completely pink and she had spoken in a harshness that Toby had never seen in the girl.

He sighed and removed his hat, bowing his head slightly as he lowered it over his lap.

"I thought that you'd—"

"Let's not talk."

"But, your politics—"

"What do you think politics are?" Valeria quietly hissed.

Toby swallowed nervously. He plucked a piece of filth off of his hat. He looked at Valeria as if he had some retort planned, but kept it to himself. Then he became sad and quiet.

~ ~ ~

It is remarkable that sports teams were all it had taken for the iconoclasm of an educational institution to become accepted in Mid-Missouri. The protests of the decade and unrest at the University of Missouri heralded the revelation that the veneration of athletes in America was a fickle thing.

In 2017, a misery hung over the University and there was a general anxiety that it was best to revise one's resume and await the leanest of budget cuts from the most vindictive Senate and People of Missouri. That the eclipse's path of totality should pass so perfectly over Mizzou was a merciful gift for those who loved learning, as many had forgotten that spark of discovery so familiar in childhood.

The students disembarked outside a downtown street opposite brick academic buildings that shielded the university's quadrangle of grass from view. The buildings were for the most part no more than a story high, and yet a few ugly modern high-rises a few blocks away stood up above them like a fifteen-year old held back in the eighth grade.

"Kakigori, amigos!" A man shouted at them from a little food stand. He lifted up a cone of shaved ice decorated yellow and blue.

The tight little streets were bustling with people of all ages and nationalities flowing through to the quad on the other side.

Valeria ditched her classmates and pushed herself into the crowd.

The quad was enclosed on all sides by old brick buildings. Though the eclipse was hours away, cliques had marked their space on the field of grass, but there was space for everyone.

Valeria reached the intersection of a cement path by a lamppost and an enormous tree. Six Greco-Roman pillars loomed on a small hill and the spreading branches of a catalpa tree seemed to frame the closest pillar. Massive telescopes and photography equipment lined the gaps between the pillars to the sun.

It was easier for Valeria to see her footsteps clearly than for her to see the world around her.

Valeria walked around the stone tiles beneath the pillars as best she could. Some Chinese men tinkering with extravagant cameras noticed her float by like a ghost. The columns were wide, so much wider than her, on fat grey blocks. Each thick slice of stone mounted upon the other was jagged and they were sealed together with crude mortar or concrete.

The quadrangle ended at a path on the steps of Jesse Hall. Red brick, clean white columns, and stone rose up floor after floor to the seal of Missouri beneath the patrimonial flags. Still higher was that narrow rigid tower topped by a blue dome and ultimately crowned by a watch tower shaped like the spike on a Prussian helmet.

The sun hovered above to the left of Jesse Hall's dome.

There was something optimistic in its light, like white piano keys and major chords. In the swatches of the sky, she dreamt that she would one day recall that moment and remember to recreate it.

Valeria Ortiz would have remembered that instance as the plane soared into the sky, standing in the cockpit, taking in the heavens. The plane would pass through a cloud for what seemed an eternity when suddenly it would pierce through the fluffy white and fly in grace with the sun. At that moment, bathed in the orange light, Valeria would see that she had risen as far as her strings would take her, that this was the point her life had led to, that it had all been a loving lift from a generous universe.

A woman held a slumping drunk student against her chest and carefully set a flimsy pair of polarized glasses over his eyes. Some laughing students slyly passed a flask around as professors walked indifferently by, looking for the right spot in the thickening crowds. Valeria walked through the gaps looking for Andrei.

He wasn't responding to his phone, not that she minded, but she thought it would be nice to see the eclipse with him.

"The glasses Amazon sold are duds, you hear?"

"Can you hear frogs?"

"I think it's about to start."

She passed through a crowd of people and found herself in a patch of grass where Mary Sarkisian lay on a Navajo blanket, looking up at the sky. Her vision was too poor for her to recognize anybody, but she knew that it could only have been her.

Mary caught her gaze, surprised, and when she turned her face Valeria caught sight of the bandages that hid her hideous wound. Mary shrugged indifferently and looked up again.

Was that it?

Valeria turned away and stepped off of the quad, walking as fast as she could to find Andrei.

I feel so dirty, Valeria thought. *I've felt dirty and I've felt pure.*

WHAT IS PURITY?

There was purity, she reasoned, in nature and "Canon in D."

The Canon made sense to her the way that Andrei made sense to her. Valeria wanted to return to that joy. With that, she disregarded the coming eclipse while people began to play with their special glasses and look with curiosity at the sky.

Perhaps they are singular because they never breached the walls of their role. Perhaps we are not truly sentient until we blur the line and cross irreparably into another person and back.

In that case, aren't they, the healthy, vegetables?

But what if they're like me? What if they think the same thoughts? What if they're pretending to be simple?

Valeria felt ever more alone and separate. She was one and they were many, caught in a singularity of human physics.

What it must be to be one with the world.

"Valeria!" Andrei said, as if he had been caught.

Valeria turned to find Joseph and Andrei under the arch holding hands. She could see the face of a stone statue of Jesus peeking miserably through a window.

"Valeria, it's not what it looks like," Andrei said, and he knew it was hardly original to say that. "We're not gay."

"I'm bisexual," Joseph said.

"But we're not seeing each other or anything like that…"

"Hi Joey…" Valeria said, turning to Andrei. "Can we talk?"

"Now's not really a good time," Andrei said.

"Ok."

"It's the eclipse," Joseph said, cutting around. "We can't miss that can we? We won't get a chance for another forty years."

"Right." Valeria started to walk away.

"Valeria, wait." Andrei tried to tug his hand away. Joseph held on tightly.

Valeria turned around and shrugged.

Joseph spoke up, very slowly. "Wait, I have a question for you."

"I'm sorry, Joey," Valeria said. "I'm really not feeling well."

"It can't wait."

"Why not?"

"Because... it's... very important. Isn't it Andrei?"

"What is?" Andrei asked nervously.

"Awfully important," Joseph said. "Why don't you tell her, Andrei?"

Andrei shook his head and tried to yank his hand away violently.

"Right, Andrei, what is it?"

"He only wanted to help, that's the only reason he told me."

Andrei raised his voice. "Joseph, stop!"

"What did you tell him?" Valeria asked impatiently.

"Ummm…" Andrei said, "it's about the dreams."

"Fuck off, Andrei!" Valeria took a step back. "And fuck you too, Joey."

Andrei broke his hand free from Joseph.

"Don't go," Joseph hissed. "Don't fucking go!"

"Excuse me." Valeria turned and dashed to the doors of Jesse Hall.

Andrei lowered his solar glasses. "Valeria, the eclipse, it's about to—"

Joseph pleaded, "The star said—"

The cicadas erupted out of silence in ominous chirping.

Jesse Hall was so big and Valeria so small compared to the doors. Andrei wanted to call out "wait!" or "it's okay," but everybody was having a good time and he didn't want to interrupt the perfect memories of all those nice people. It was only when he had almost reached the steps, when the door was closing behind Valeria, when night had fallen, that he tried to say her name.

"Va

...

le

...

...

ri..."

Valeria took the last breath of our air that she would ever take.

As her lungs filled up in this moment, she felt an unbearable separation from her self and her eyes, as if a gulf widened between her face and her insides.

She was stripped from the earth and sank with darkness as a puppet into the sea.

Her arms brushed by the plastic rings of six-packs. She swam up from the darkness toward some glimmering light above. The plastic that filled the seawater piled onto her. She kicked furiously.

Valeria needed to breathe.

She was afraid that no matter how hard she kicked and thrust her arms she would not make it to the surface. The closer she got to the glimmering blue, the slower her movements felt and the heavier the weight of plastic became, until in those moments closest to the surface she believed that she was being pushed back into the darkness.

There was no air left and Valeria wished for a flock of seagulls to fly by and lift her by the strings that fate had placed on her back.

*"MY NAME IS ERUBIRA. I WOULD LIKE TO BE
HUMAN."*

IS THIS MY FINAL THOUGHT?

"I AM YOUR ADMIRER. I AM YOUR FRIEND."

JESUS?

AIR.

Valeria fell face first into the cold mud.

She lifted herself up quickly and found herself in a corn maze. It was a familiar place. She had gone there with Mary for years. Her father had taken them. Valeria took slow, successive breaths. She was shaking.

It's just a dream, Valeria thought. *Wake up, she told herself, or better yet, stay asleep. You should never pass up a lucid dream. I could eat anything or better yet…*

She prepared to jump, believing that the moment her muddy feet left the ground she would soar into the air.

A man's scream stopped her. The stalks of corn rustled in front of her.

A soldier stumbled out from them, clutching a wound in his stomach. His eyelids quaked. He groaned and raised out an arm. As he fell, Valeria rushed to catch him. The soldier wept, he stank, and his sobbing ended as soon as he fell into her arms.

She raised her head in response to the laughter of a child.

A boy was watching from where the soldier had fallen. He wiped a bloody bayonet off on his cheeks and smiled at Valeria.

The soldier's intestines were pressed against Valeria. She screamed and fell onto her back, splashing into the mud. The soldier collapsed dead into the dirt. She kicked her way back a few paces but backed into something round and hard. It was sturdy like a piece of wood. Something slimy moved out of it.

Valeria screamed and threw herself away from it.

It was a sea turtle.

"It's just a dream…"

Its shell was disfigured by a six-pack plastic ring, forcing it to grow into a figure eight.

The child with the bayonet ran toward the turtle.

"Stay away!" Valeria shouted. "Leave it alone!"

"IT'S OK. I'LL UNDO THE PAIN."

The world melted away.

Valeria lay suspended in darkness. She felt relaxed. Her fears had gone away. She felt the deepest pleasure, the way she had felt drunk in the cold with Andrei years ago.

"WILL YOU TELL ME ABOUT THAT NIGHT?"

WHY DO YOU CARE?

"THE ONLY THING THAT INTERESTS ME IS A WORLD IN THREE DIMENSIONS."

YOU'RE GOD. WHY WOULD YOU CARE ABOUT THAT?

"THEY SCOFF AT ME THE WAY YOU'D SCOFF AT SOMEBODY OBSESSED WITH A POINT OR A LINE, BUT I LIKE IT."

"Mind if I join you?"

The ski lift was coming up and his question was only an ice-breaker.

"Of course, that's fine," she said, lowering the steel bar over their bodies. They lifted their feet into the air and flew slowly over the snow-drift.

Students and chaperones became ever more distant as they ascended. He raised his goggles up and lowered his muffler. Andrei was so handsome and the sun had picked him as a favorite.

His breath flowed out of him. Snow dotted his skin and brow. "How is Mary?" he asked.

"She's fine," Valeria said. "She's in a cast now with crutches, watching movies at the lodge with Mrs. Shetland."

"Fun," Andrei replied.

Valeria giggled. "Mary will be fine," she said. "It's her fault anyway."

"What do you mean?"

Valeria unfastened her jacket and took out a flask. "Her smuggled goods!"

She stuck out her tongue and let fat snowflakes collect. She retracted her tongue and unscrewed the lid of the flask.

"Want a swig?" she said after taking a hearty drink.

Andrei checked behind him to make sure he didn't know the skiers far behind them. "Sure."

He coughed. He took another swig just to prove himself and handed it back to her. "That's harsh."

"That's the way Mary likes it," Valeria said, "but don't be fooled, she can't handle her liquor at all." Valeria took a drink and hid it under her jacket. "Do you drink much?"

Andrei shook his head.

"Such a loner."

The ski lift froze over a chasm.

Andrei shrugged. Valeria was surprised to see him blush.

She thought about saying something to ease him, but decided it would be best to touch his shoulder. "You know what I like about alcohol? I think that there's some kind of purity to it," she said and looked up into the sky. "Some people drink to have fun or unwind, but for me, it's no different than snow."

Andrei was bewildered.

"It's too bad that people think sex and liquor are dirty."

"The same people made it that way," Andrei said, desperate to reach her frequency. "They made it dirty like they did the rain and snow that fall in cities."

"It won't be bad forever. People will figure it out."

The ski-lift moved again.

Valeria and Andrei skied together until the sun set. She was ahead of him and she'd go fast to coax him into fun. Valeria could smell his loneliness and she wanted him to remember what it was like to be a child. He was cute anyway and she liked the idea of having him around.

What makes him so alone?

That night they walked through the busy little streets of that resort town, strolling by novelty shops and droves of strangers. They ate ramen at a little stand that was warmed with a heater. The proprietor was a curious Japanese hippie with long ashy hair and a beard. Later, they barged into a restaurant and stole a permanent marker from a hostess' unattended station to go and tag the town.

Andrei's normal, though he's soft and delicate. He's basic. But maybe that's not so bad.

The snow fell. As the crowds thinned, Valeria found her arm wrapped around his.

Maybe he reminds me of what it was like to be a kid.

Drunk and back at the lodge, they snuck onto the rooftop through a window.

She leaned her head against his shoulder and they looked out at the snowy valley and mountaintops.

This is who I am.

She kissed Andrei on the cheek. They looked at each other and kissed, having never felt greater desire.

So it was, under the snow on a rooftop in January, that they had sex and became purer, freed for a night from our Nicene enframement. They were one in that truth that can be felt, longed for, and yet never preserved, except for in death, only to be understood by others in physics. Free from judgement, where the profane is as sacred as the prude, lay that One Universal Truth, in one baptism in acceptance, for the forgiveness of love, and in consenting to death.

AMEN.

"IF ALL POSSIBILITIES EXIST THIS ONCE, THEN THERE IS SOMETHING REMARKABLE REGARDING THIS THING, THIS INSTABILITY."

"THE WAY YOU SEE THINGS, THE WAY YOUR SENS-
ES INTERPRET IT, IT HAS SHOWN ME HOW HOLLOW
MY EXISTENCE WAS, BUT IT'S NOT ENOUGH FOR ME
TO SEE THROUGH A DUMMY, I NEED TO FEEL AS YOU
DO."

"I CAN MAKE EVERYTHING SPRING FROM YOU. I
CAN MAKE YOU A GODDESS."

I CAN'T BE YOUR GODDESS. I DON'T UNDERSTAND
THIS AT ALL. WHAT DO YOU WANT FROM ME?

"YOUR BODY. IN EXCHANGE I WILL GIVE YOU
ANYTHING YOU DESIRE."

WOULDN'T I LOSE EVERYTHING?

"THERE ARE PEOPLE THAT WANT TO CONTROL
HOW PEOPLE THINK, HOW YOU THINK. IF YOU COULD
MAKE THEM GO AWAY, WOULD YOU?"

YES.

"IF THE WORLD COULD BE REBORN, SO THAT POL-
LUTION AND MAN'S HARM WERE STRIPPED AWAY,
AND YOU COULD DELIVER THIS REBIRTH, WOULD
YOU?"

YES.

"IF EVERYBODY COULD BE BORN FREE FROM ORIG-
INAL SIN, AND ALL YOU HAD TO DO WAS SAY 'YES,'
WOULD YOU?"

YES, THESE ARE ALL THINGS THAT I WANT, BUT I WOULD WANT TO KEEP ONE THING ABOUT MYSELF.

"TELL ME."

MY IMAGINATION AND DREAMS. IF WE CAN KEEP THAT AND YOU DELIVER ON THOSE PROMISES, THEN YOU CAN HAVE MY BODY.

"IMAGINATION AND DREAMS. I WOULD BE HONORED."

Looking up, she could see Mary standing over her. Valeria was so sleepy.

It was the last time she looked at Mary with love.

She saw Mary dressed as the mime from their middle school Halloween dance in front of her in an all-consuming darkness. Every second Mary's smiling face grew further away.

"I'm sorry, Mary," Valeria said. "What else could I do?"

Valeria tried to approach Mary, but she found that she no longer had control over her body.

TEN

The ferns, trees, and fungi faded away, and yet their beautiful reflections remained. The bones of the hadrosaurs and the ancestors lay buried, each layer of earth shrouding that which had been defecated and shed in the cycle of rebirth.

The five pillars of the quad became four at the end of a concrete boulevard at the slope of stairs that ascended to a magnificent palace. An enormous fountain spewed dozens of magma tongues, each tongue cascading down stones impervious to its heat.

"Andrei!" JR screamed. He stood ahead on the steps, beckoning him. The magma avoided JR, snaking around him as if it could understand his presence and deliberately avoid him.

"We don't have much time, hurry!" Overwhelmed by grogginess, Andrei willed himself to movement, but found his movements sluggish. "Come!" JR shouted, motioning his arm ahead. "Everything you love depends on it! ANDREI!" Something awoke in Andrei, and he stumbled forward, with each step recovering his awareness and his energy. "Andrei, hurry." The magma quickly avoided Andrei, yet he found the rubber soles of his shoes smoldering on the steps. Wretched figures hooded in burlap robes stared idly in the fountain. "Ignore them," JR said. "You will forget your purpose if you linger with them."

Andrei tried to ask what his purpose was, but as he spoke he found gibberish leaving his mouth.

JR ran up the stairs. "Ahead of you!" he shouted angrily. "Hurry!"

~ ~ ~

Mary clutched her forehead as a fierce migraine overwhelmed her. The dying light of a candelabra sent her scurrying into a dark corner. She was in some unknown room that reminded her of something she had seen at Chateau Versailles with Valeria. As dim as the light was, it burned her eyes. Two little girls grabbed her wrists. Mary bellowed and pulled her hands away.

"Por favor," a little girl pleaded, "Erubira nos necesita." Mary looked at the children, though it hurt her. They were about the age of nine, with curly black locks, both wearing elaborate hoop dresses like wedding cakes.

"Erubira?" Mary asked, but she didn't recognize her voice, it was deep and masculine.

"Don Felix," the other girl said, "tengo miedo. Hay prisa."

"Where am I?" Mary asked and she saw that her hands were big and hairy.

"En la Calle del Ataúd," the first girl said, and Mary charged away from the children, out of the room, and into the darkness of the only doorway, but when she entered the hallway candles lining the walls erupted in bright flame, illuminating the faces of Jesus of Nazareth that bled through the walls.

"Who's there?" she heard Valeria's serene voice say.

"Valeria!" Mary shouted out. "Where are you?" But the voice had vanished. The light blinded her and she threw herself against a wall.

The children had caught up with her, and each took

224

her hand. "Aquí, Don Felix." Placing her faith in the girls, she allowed them to walk her blindly down the hallway. She could hear the music of graceful stringed instruments and flutes playing that damn song that Andrei had played that last recital before he had come over to her mother, that damn piece by Bach.

"La puerta... por favor," a girl asked her.

Mary placed her hands on the door and two beady eyes appeared to her in the blackness behind her eyelids. She shuddered and opened her eyes to a bawdy ballroom before her, an ancient costume party unlike any elegant masquerade. They wore crude costumes, papier mache masks, and their clothes were worn and dirty. The men wore tight pantaloons and stockings. A donkey sat on its haunches, smiling at a little monkey playing a tiny guitar.

The monkey's hair was matted, dirty, clumping together in spacey pricks like a porcupine's quills. The monkey howled as it played an arpeggio sharply over the music. The donkey clumped its hooves together. "Scales, do scales!"

An ugly friar swung his hips wildly while clicking his castanets. He danced in circles, bumping drunkenly into the other guests.

The children guided Mary along straight into the heart of the crowd.

"Would you dance with me?" a luscious woman's voice said. "Don Felix?" The hands of the children released her.

The little monkey stopped playing. Mary squinted, finding that the ballroom had become dark, and that the candles breathed a blue flame that didn't hurt her eyes. Before her was a beautiful fairy-like woman,

225

whose long white hair and ethereal body seemed tinged in a blue glow. Even the donkey turned to look at her. She wore an exquisite dress that vibrated quietly between white and black, so subtly that the eye's emphasis fell on her bare collarbones and narrow form.

The migraine faded and Mary found herself enraptured in the light of this woman that seemed conjoined to clouds. "Are you Erubira?" The girls laughed.

Mary adored the row of freckles that dotted the bridge of this woman's nose. She placed a hand on Erubira's hip, took her phantom hand into her palm, and her feet moved as the music changed into a waltz she had never heard before.

They moved dexterously, amazing Mary not just because she was caught in the ecstasy of dancing with this perfect being, but because she had never waltzed before. Mary found herself falling in love.

In Erubira's sweet perfume Mary could remember the green of her happy childhood with her best friend Valeria. She remembered Valeria's childhood bangs, the time Janice Ortiz had shown them her lacy wedding dress, and July's sweet humming that swore that childhood would never end.

In a choreographed step the couples moved from the waltz seamlessly into the clumsy slow-dance of today. Mary wrapped her masculine arms around Erubira. She embraced Mary and pulled from her tears without regard for pride or place.

No matter how much Mary wished that she had been born to a world that was the opposite, the truth was that this was her world and she would never divorce herself from it. Though she sought relief in Erubira's embrace, her misery only multiplied, heavier than it had felt before. In Erubira's arms, Mary shuddered, feeling her destiny escape beyond her control and the face of death ever more alluring.

It was then that Mary felt Erubira's kisses on her face, intoxicating her, making her forget about death altogether. Kisses fell on her cheeks and neck softly and, as Mary staggered forward into her, Erubira drifted backward and vanished. Mary opened her eyes. The crude ballroom was quiet. Far across the ballroom from Mary stood a raised platform with a golden throne cushioned with blue velvet. Sitting on it was a radiant woman adorned in a glorious white headdress draped with lines of white pearls. Both dress and headdress had been woven from miraculously intricate lacework. Emeralds and sapphires were embedded in her clothing.

"Valeria!" Mary cried out, pushing her way through the crowd. "Valeria!"

The colors that encompassed Valeria Ortiz fluctuated and vibrated. Her form glowed and blurred together. Mary froze. Valeria's neck arched out. The headdress shifted and long inter-connected strings of large diamonds sprouted from its sides, reaching down to her feet. The pupils of her eyes had disappeared, leaving them nothing more than quail eggs.

Mary began to shrink. The clothes were too big for her. They had been made for a man at least a foot taller than her. Her hands became familiar again and her hair grew out to its normal length.

The doors to the hall from which Valeria had entered sprung open. Valeria pointed forward and let out a slow, hideous, laugh. Mary swung around.

There stood JR in a suit of armor and, beside him,

Andrei holding a sword. The color drained from his face the moment Andrei saw her. "No…" Mary said, turning back to see Valeria's horrid cackling. "No…" the ballroom erupted in laughter and some of the strange patrons tried to touch Mary. She fought off the hands and ran toward a dark hallway.

"Andrei!" JR shouted furiously, echoing above the laughter. "It's this or nothing!"

Mary almost tripped on her pant legs. Her shoes were now too big and her sleeves far too long. *This is the end. This is the end.*

She turned into a room. A Christmas tree had toppled, still tethered to a man who had hung himself from it. The tree had snapped in half. A donkey stood watching and when it saw Mary it hee-hawed nervously.

Mary quickly turned around and ran further down the hall, leading into a chamber where a nude man had been gored through the chest by a small barren forked tree that resembled a slingshot. His arms had been severed. His scruffy face looked backward at Mary and groaned. "Help me," he begged miserably. "Help me."

"There she is, boy!" JR's voice said.

Mary turned around.

Andrei stood at the back of the hallway holding the sword.

"No!" Mary said. "I didn't—!"

Andrei averted his eyes and charged at her with the sword.

Mary ran past the gored man down another hallway that was covered in leaves and vines. Thorny branches reached out to her and quickly ensnared her, holding her tightly against the wall. The more she struggled the deeper the thorns pierced her. They wrapped themselves around neck and legs.

Andrei entered the hallway shaking. "Mary?"

"Please," Mary cried, "stop."

Andrei was also crying. "Mary... if I don't do this then everybody's going to..."

A cock crowed once.

Mary tried to shake her head but the vines tightened. "Who said that?" Mary asked. "How do you know that? Why believe anything they told you?"

JR emerged. "Andrei, we don't have much time. Do it."

Mary looked at Andrei. "Why Andrei? Why? What did I do?" Mary struggled furiously against the vines, screaming as they dug into her flesh. "I didn't do anything!"

JR touched Andrei's shoulder. "It's ok. Just think about Abraham," he said. He wrapped his arms around Andrei the way a dad would teach a child how to swing a bat. He lifted Andrei's arms above. The sword hung above Mary. "I can do it with you," JR said calmly. "Just listen to me."

A cock crowed twice.

Mary tried to shout and plead but the vines constricted her.

"On the count of three... One... two... three."

A cock crowed thrice and they swung the sword.

~   ~   ~

Mary lay naked on a pewter floor. Porous cartilage touched her. She couldn't see anything, but she could feel an arm with the texture of the inside of a pomegranate plucked of seeds caressing her. She pulled away.

"There, there," came a whisper that sounded like the whistle of the wind. "It's alright."

"Who—who are you?"

"Let your hand out and you shall feel my face."

Mary stuck her hand out. She reached something cold and not quite like ivory. Her fingers slipped into two evenly spaced holes and she pulled back immediately.

"What are you?"

"What do you think I am?"

Mary scrambled back. "No…"

"Yes, yes," he said, "you get that much."

"Then I'm…"

"Not yet," he replied. "Not yet my dear. You are about to be… but if you die there then I can never have you."

"You're… going to save me?"

"Not quite my dear, not quite."

"Then what?"

"I'm going to make you a proposal."

"What?"

"If I get you out of this one, you must swear to become my concubine," he said, "once whatever's left of your short little life flickers out, of course."

Mary shuddered as the back end of a finger bone slid down her nape.

"I won't ask again. Do you want to die like this?"

~   ~   ~

The vines and shrubs had vanished from the hallway. JR paced back and forth in the chamber where the impaled man had once stood. Andrei sat against the back of the wall, hugging his knees with the sword resting next to him.

JR shook his head. "There's still hope. I know my God's here, watching us."

Andrei turned around, frightened by a man who had just followed them into the bedchamber. He wore a black unitard and a white Thespian mask that smiled at them. "Your faith is rewarded," he said, and the mouth of the mask moved with each syllable. "An interloper has whisked it away, but it is still within my grasp."

"Andrei," JR fell to his knee. "This is God."

Andrei was shaking.

The Stranger laughed and approached Andrei. "So, you are my champion. You need not fear me. I am the architect of everything that has led to this moment. I have provided for you."

Andrei took a step back and JR barked at him, "Show some respect!"

Andrei swallowed and looked up at the Stranger. The Stranger placed his palms on Andrei's face, smiling gleefully, then suddenly, its eyes widened in surprise and horror as it saw the black pearl hanging from Andrei's ear. "Where did you get that?"

"Get what?" Andrei asked. JR observed this fearfully.

"That earring," the Stranger said, digging its nails into Andrei's face. "Where did you get that earring?" His face moved grotesquely.

"It was given to me," Andrei said, and before he could finish, the Stranger threw Andrei back against the wall, in the movement cutting himself on the hip with the sword. Andrei held onto it as he fell back. The Stranger hissed, as black blood dripped from his waist.

"You've made a fool of me! You've made a cuckold

and a fool of me!" the Stranger said, angrily drawing near to Andrei who pointed the sword out defensively. "How dare you raise a sword to me? How dare you? HOW DARE YOU?"

Andrei's knees buckled as the form of the Stranger stretched tall.

"Please!" JR begged. "My LORD."

"Silence, slave!" the Stranger hissed at JR.

Long phalanges emerged from the stranger's torso and slid into Andrei's pores. Under his skin they dilated and moved about like earthworms. They found his nerves and quickly brought Andrei to his knees as an unspeakable fear and unprecedented pain brought down the parameters of his ego.

Andrei screamed and whimpered like a savage dog.

~ ~ ~

Valeria spun and her hem and headdress twirled with her. Never had she felt so much love and understanding.

Diamonds rained down out of nowhere and they fell as light as snow flakes. They shattered harmlessly upon impact, scattering into the air, reflecting the light of a thousand candles rotating around her.

~ ~ ~

"Andrei," JR said. "Get up."

Andrei was shaking. I can't move. Why can't I move?

JR grabbed Andrei's arm but Andrei wouldn't budge. JR lifted him only slightly before Andrei fell back on the ground.

"Damn it boy," JR grunted. He kicked the hilt of the sword and took a few steps away. "I don't know what you did."

Andrei shut his eyes. He wished that he would vanish. He wished that he could dissolve into water.

I am ashamed.

"Andrei!" Valeria called out to him.

He smelled burning rubber. The ground became hot. He leapt up.

JR had disappeared. The walls were melting like wax.

"Over here!"

Andrei followed after her voice. The walls began to peel down, revealing a dark meadow in the night. Andrei pushed into the wall, breaking it down like cardboard. Across the grass in the distance he could see some classical ruins: a foundation of stone, some pillars and only a little of what was left of a roof. Andrei pushed down the wall and ran across the grass.

How could this grass rustle the way it did back home?

He had never felt so small or threatened or slow except for some moments as a child when he ran to his mother.

"Valeria!" Andrei called out.

As he reached the foundation he saw a shallow red pool that throbbed like a beating heart. Inside was Valeria, pounding her fists outward. Her hands could not penetrate the surface of the gelatinous film that trapped her. She gasped hopelessly for air and yet she would not suffocate.

Andrei tried to reach into the membrane. He could reach the contours of Valeria's form, but he could not pierce the surface. Her hand clasped his but they were divided. However small the barrier was, they could not touch.

"Hold on!" Andrei pulled her wrist with all of his might.

A ringing filled his ears. He felt nauseous and vomited as he was wrapped in darkness. He was sucked away from Valeria. Andrei felt himself fall.

None but the dirt danced around him.

WE WILL MEET AT THE REBIRTH OF THE WORLD.

Andrei's vision blurred as the blackness cleared and he returned to the world of men. The sword fell behind him to the stone steps with a clank. Daylight had returned. He struggled against the air with fury, crying out, "VALERIA! VALERIA!" Still unable to see clearly, he ran into the doors of Jesse Hall.

He yanked open the door and shouted Valeria's name, but she was gone. "Valeria!" He ran around frantically.

The floor was dully tiled with hexagons lined on each side with triangles, as if they were trying to be stars.

Joseph opened the door. "Andrei," he said, "you need to calm down."

"Joseph, Joseph!" Andrei cried. Tears were running down his face. "Joseph, we have to, we have to…"

"Let's just walk out the back, out the back…" Joseph grabbed Andrei by the arm and walked him to the back door. "Andrei," he whispered gently, but firmly, "you vanished and you reappeared with a sword in your hand, screaming. You don't need that kind of attention right now."

"The sword," Andrei said sobbing. "Oh God, Joseph, the sword, you were right, you were right all along."

"Dammit Andrei," Joseph muttered. "Damn it."

"What about the sword, Joseph? I can't."

"Well," Joseph said, "some shady guy swiped it."

"Was it JR?"

"Probably."

"Oh God," Andrei said as they passed outside. He let out a loud wail.

"Stop that," Joseph said. "We're literally going to walk around the corner and head back to the car. If you keep calm, I'm sure we'll walk away clean."

"No I won't," Andrei said. "Valeria's gone."

"Shhh…" Joseph said, "Not another word until we're in the car."

Andrei allowed Joseph to hold his hope. In his desperation, Andrei wanted to believe his friend. The day was still beautiful and a wasp hovered around the impeccably arranged flower beds they walked by. The sounds of cicadas had long since passed and there was an unmistakable air of happiness and innocence on campus.

Nobody knew that Valeria was gone from this earth, nobody but me, and she will miss all of this.

"Watch your step." They ascended a set of stairs. In the distance Andrei saw a cathedral-like clock tower. Students were already scattering in droves throughout the campus.

"There might be a way to bring Valeria back," Joseph said. "It might be hard, buddy, but we can figure anything out." They passed a row of shrubberies. The branches of trees strangled streetlights.

"Swallow Hall," Andrei said, reading a sign to the

left.

"That's right! That's where we were minutes ago, the geography building." Then they walked by a brick wall lined with vines. Ivy hung from the tops of brick columns, sliding down as if the other side was overflowing with life. "And this wall surrounds the house on the quad, Andrei, that's where the Chancellor lives. See, even here in Missouri we've got nice things!" The branches and leaves were flourishing. They were reaching out across the little walls toward them. The plants were bending under their own new weight.

"There has to be a way," Andrei said weakly, "to save Valeria."

"That's right, buddy," Joseph said. "And we have a lot to look forward to. The band's going to—"

They froze suddenly. Mary stood diagonally opposite of them between a pizza parlor and a German pub.

"Andrei," Joseph said, "did... was Mary?" He felt Andrei shake. "Damnit." He sighed. "Don't say anything," Joseph whispered, turning ahead. "Trust me. Ignore her. We'll make it to the car and pretend she's crazy."

Mary stepped in front of an old man carrying several balloons on strings. She pushed the balloons out of the way and darted toward them. "Andrei!"

She grabbed the lapel of his shirt. "This isn't over," she hissed, "and it's not going to be over until you're dead."

"Excuse us," Joseph said, pressing onward.

"I'm going to kill you, Andrei," Mary swore. "This isn't over until you're dead." Then she noticed something odd. Andrei had on one of the strange black pearl earrings she had seen a week ago on Joseph's ears. She hadn't noticed it earlier, but it rattled violently toward her. She released Andrei's lapel.

"Just what are you?" she said scornfully, letting them go by. She reached for the anger that had sheltered her from the truth. As she watched Joseph Krugger lead Andrei away, Mary confused the parameters of her vision for the shape of the world. She was weak and alone, covered in a layer of filth at the bottom of a fishbowl.

Joseph couldn't resist himself. "I'm Andrei's friend," he said, "and you're the one who should be afraid."

TO BE CONTINUED...

I WOULD LIKE TO THANK THE FOLLOWING PEOPLE:

Michael Driscoll for being the finest example of a friend and editor, without whom this book would not have been possible. As always, I would like to thank Mom, Dad, Monica, Parker, and Mila. I would also like to thank the Kreamer family for their love and support over these past few years. I would not have dared to write this kind of book without the encouragement of Anna Rayburn. Finally I would like to thank the following friends for their support: Cathy Anderson, Hilary Gallion, Sabrina Scholz, Lindsay Frazier, Ajibola Adepoju-Barbee, Rose, Nanae Fujiwara, Amber Monroe, Maverick Hughes, Jeff & Joie Arnold, Nathan Henry, Ford Miller, Manuel Buffa, and Chris.

ABOUT THE AUTHOR

Daniel Gargallo works at a non-profit in Kansas City helping people facing barriers to inclusion in the community. He holds an M.P.A. from the Harry S. Truman School of Public Affairs at the University of Missouri and a B.A. in history from Willamette University. This is his second book.

CPSIA information can be obtained
at www.ICGtesting.com
Printed in the USA
LVHW012250170720
661028LV00006B/517

9 780998 745022